THE CAPTAIN'S JOURNEY

ANITA LORENE SMITH

iUniverse, Inc.
Bloomington

The Captain's Journey

iUniverse books may be ordered through booksellers or by contacting:

iUniverse
1663 Liberty Drive
Bloomington, IN 47403
www.iuniverse.com
1-800-Authors (1-800-288-4677)

ISBN: 978-1-4759-3567-7 (sc)
ISBN: 978-1-4759-3568-4 (ebk)

Printed in the United States of America

iUniverse rev. date: 07/12/2012

The captain lowered Echo to a sitting position and wrapped a Navajo blanket around both of them. Echo's bedroll and blanket had given her more thickness, but she was warm all of a sudden with the Navajo blanket and the captain's body warmth. She stopped shivering and her head cleared. Still, something about the cave felt eerie. She hadn't noticed it before. Briefly, she wondered if it was something in the stew. She mentioned her strange feeling to the captain. The captain just shook her head slowly. "Something feels different to me too. I don't know the cause though."

Table of Contents

Acknowledgements

Thanks to my sister, Susan Contor, my friend, Jennifer Starr, and my former writing instructor, Cynthia Ward, for reviewing my manuscript and making helpful suggestions. Thanks also to Betty Holland for help with Spanish translations.

Chapter 1
The Cave

Echo watched while the younger Mexican backed the deuce-and-a-half into the cave. The entrance was just barely high and wide enough for the old beat up troop transport. Outside the cave with Echo were the older Mexican man and the captain's brother, Dean. The two men were motioning this way and that for the driver to adjust his wheels, move forward, then move back. Echo caught herself holding her breath as the truck barely missed hitting the side of the cave opening near where she was standing. Finally, the vehicle backed in all the way, and Echo let out a sigh of relief. The two men and Echo then went running into the cave to join the captain and the stray girl they'd found.

Inside, the cave was spacious with a high ceiling. Everything in the cave was composed of light tan rock. Looking around, Echo noticed a few faint drawings on the walls, and on the ceiling were numerous hooks embedded into the rock. People had stayed here before.

The welcome relief of shade and coolness hit Echo right away. She sat on a rock near Captain Stewart, who was already undoing her pack and removing supplies. The girl just sat and watched and said nothing, looking as frightened as when they'd found her outside a storefront in the small, dusty town not far from where they were now.

The captain stood up and motioned Echo toward the now parked truck. "Let's start unloading." Echo responded by running toward the truck, but her first priority was a drink of water.

"We've got enough until tomorrow night if we ration," Dean said as Echo poured herself a cup from the tap. She wanted more but she'd wait.

The cave had a large fire pit in the middle, but since they were in the high desert along a mountain road, there was no kindling to be found. Dean produced several chunks of firewood from the truck, and the younger Mexican poured some flammable fluid over it. The fire sprang to life with a whoof.

The older Mexican brought out a large kettle and proceeded to make a stew, chopping vegetables, husking corn, and stirring. Dean turned to Echo and the captain. "Won't be ready for about an hour. Might as well get some rest."

On each side of the cavernous cave were plate-like depressions just the right size for making beds. Echo wondered if someone had carved out the depressions or if they were natural. The captain was already laying out a blanket in one of the depressions. She tossed a blanket to Echo and one to the girl, who just stood there holding it. The captain looked at Echo as if to say, help her. Echo dropped her own blanket and went to help the girl.

"This is where you'll sleep," Echo motioned to the girl. She probably doesn't speak English, Echo thought. Evidently, the girl understood because she picked up the blanket and moved it closer to the fire pit, then laid out the blanket in a smaller depression. She then put on her poncho and sat cross-legged staring into the fire and rocked herself forward and back.

Echo shrugged and came back to her own blanket, laid it out neatly and sat down. The captain was sitting with her feet dangling off the short ledge in front of her. "I wonder how old she is," Echo said.

"I'd say around eleven or twelve," the captain replied.

"Wonder what happened to her."

"Later I'm going to see if one of the Mexican guys can get her talking. She might only be able to speak Spanish."

"Yeah, good idea." Echo yawned.

"We'll need more blankets out of the truck. It's going to get cold tonight."

"What about our heat globes? They should keep us warm."

"We'll use them but we'll still need more blankets," the captain said.

Echo lay down on her back using her wadded up jacket as a pillow. She felt all her muscles relax. In a few minutes, she closed her eyes, but as soon as she did, nature called. Darn, I'm going to have to go outside in that hot sun, she thought. At least it was low in the sky.

"Where you go?" said the older Mexican in his broken English.

"Out," Echo said, hoping he would understand.

It must have dawned on him what Echo was up to. "No, no, Señorita." He pointed toward the back of the cave where the truck was parked. "Toilet back there. Come."

Echo was amazed to find a modern disintegrator toilet tucked in a semi-private corner of the cave. The small area even had a curtain, warn though it was, and a solar-powered sonic hand sanitizer. A hole in the ceiling allowed the sun to stream through, Echo imagined, probably two to three hours at midday. Someone had even left a couple rolls of tissue. She wondered if the dwellers of this cave would return any time to find it occupied by them—fugitives. They weren't fugitives from the law, but fugitives on the run from a powerful outlaw, who was free. It didn't seem right, but here they were.

Echo took her time getting back to her blanket. She studied the illustrations of people and donkeys on the walls. A few coyotes were scratched into the rock as an afterthought, as if a child illustrated them. The people and donkeys carrying packs looked more carefully etched, as if the artist or artists took their time and were more skilled.

The men were busy chopping carrots, husking corn, shelling peas, and dicing potatoes, then tossing them into a big black pot that was secured over the fire pit by a tripod. Echo didn't offer to help and they didn't ask for her help. She was beat. The girl continued sitting cross-legged, staring into the fire.

It seemed as if Echo had only dozed off for a few minutes when she heard Dean's voice yell, "Come and get it." She slowly woke to the enticing odor of hot spices and fragrant food. Her stomach growled. She hadn't eaten anything since early morning.

They all gathered around the pit. A stack of ceramic bowls sat next to the kettle. The older Mexican brought some large spoons and was the first to ladle out a bowl of stew. At first, Echo thought he was being presumptuous by going first, but then she saw him take the bowl and spoon over to the girl, who sat silently, close to the kettle.

"This hot. Be careful," he told her. She looked at him questioningly with her dirty face. He repeated himself, Echo assumed, in Spanish. She seemed to understand and took the bowl. Blowing on the steaming stew, she sampled a bite. Echo could tell she was hungry. They all were. The girl tried to eat fast, but that was impossible until the stew cooled down.

"Here," Dean said as he extended a plate of what looked like buttered French bread to the young Mexican, who then offered a piece to the girl. She grabbed a large hunk and began to stuff it into her mouth, intermittently dunking it into the stew to soften it. The rest of them took stew and bread and tried not to eat as ravenously as the girl. The stew had a chicken broth base and was the tastiest thing Echo had eaten in a very long time.

They all ate for a while, silent except for the clanking of spoons against bowls and occasional slurping of stew. Once everyone's hunger was satisfied, Echo learned the young Mexican's name was Jamey and the older one's name was Amando. No one could get the girl to tell them her name. Maybe in time.

"How long do you think it'll take us to get to Spike, Dean?" the captain asked.

"Hard to tell. If we make it to the summit without any mishaps, and if the roads are okay, and if we don't get shot at by our pursuers, maybe two hours."

The captain nodded thoughtfully then said, "I appreciate everyone's help." She made eye contact with each of them except the girl, who was staring into her empty bowl. "I mean it."

Dean spoke up after an awkward silence. "I don't know about everyone else, but I'm always game for a new adventure."

"You bet," Echo said. Jamey and Amando nodded agreement.

The fire was dying down, and the cave grew darker. Only a sliver of sunlight beamed through the cave entrance. All of a sudden, Echo felt a chill go through her.

Dean stood. "Let's not waste water doing the dishes. Everyone just stack them up over here."

Then the captain stood. "Thanks for taking care of dinner guys. We'll straighten things up."

After Echo and the captain stacked the dishes in a box and set the kettle aside, Echo followed her to the truck to fetch the sleeping bags. They didn't have one for the girl. And they didn't have any pillows at all. They would have to lie on blankets and hope they had enough to keep them warm.

As soon as the sun was gone, Amando and Jamey unfolded a ladder and hung a large woolen olive drab blanket over the opening of the cave. Now Echo knew what the built-in hooks were for. Those on the ceiling were probably for separating the cave into areas for privacy in case large groups or families stayed there.

Echo desperately wanted a shower. After traveling all day in triple digit Fahrenheit temperatures through a dusty desert in the back of a truck, she felt like flypaper coated with sand. In the toilet room, she removed her mismatched fatigues and wiped her body as best she could with her bandana. She had only one change of clothes with her, and she was saving them.

Her bag and blankets were laid out a few feet from the captain's. The captain, of course, wouldn't sleep as much as the others because of her brain implant. The whole reason they were here was that they were running from her ex-boyfriend's kidnappers, who were trying to abduct her. Jump Davis had become obsessed with capturing her. Echo didn't know for sure, but she thought he might be after her implant to copy its design for his company. But she hoped to be rid of the thing safely, by a special procedure in Canada, which was where they were headed. Echo wondered if the captain felt bad about once trusting Davis. Echo would. But he was a sly character, arranging for the death of an older couple on Mars as well as trying to get the captain to swap out her implant for an exploding one—one he had promised would give her even more longevity.

Echo lay down on her bedroll and sighed. It was all too much for her brain to handle right now, anyway. She needed to turn off her thoughts and sleep. If only she could.

The desert cooked in the daytime but chilled way down at night. It was completely dark outside now, and once the fire pit had gone out, only a few heat globes lit the cave. Echo could barely make out the men across the pit on the opposite side. Dean planted a few more heat globes near the girl and lined some up on the way to the facility. They would likely go out before dawn. Then they would need recharging in the sun on the way to Spike. But hopefully, they wouldn't be needed tomorrow night. Hopefully they would find a hotel with real beds and a real shower.

Echo was a fool to think she would go to sleep right away. She might as well have had an implant in *her* head. For some reason, as she was staring at the cave's ceiling, her mind flashed back to her year on the spaceship. They'd gone to the asteroid belt to deliver geologists to find and mine uzerium, the precious energy producing metal first found on Mars. The venture was overwhelmingly successful, but after a couple of months out, Echo had become extremely claustrophobic, which didn't make any sense. The ship was huge and had lots of diversions like a micro-gravity gymnasium, a full-featured kitchen, a VR game room, and an entertainment center. The bridge had a full view of the outside in any designated direction. The quarters were spacious as far as a ship was concerned, with viewscreens that could display Earth nature scenes.

On that mission, the captain and Echo, along with several other crewmembers, would shuttle over to one of the asteroids on a weekly basis. Echo thought it was the only thing that kept her sane. She slept a lot to escape the reality of not being on Earth. She thought it eventually got to everyone—some just showed it more than others. It was ironic really—all her life Echo had dreamed of going to space. Going to Mars and the moon hadn't bothered her except for her six-month work assignment on the moon. But she could see the Earth from the moon and knew home was only a few hours away. On Mars she had seen her father, but it was on Mars that he had also died. What was she doing, thinking about all this stuff now? She just wanted to turn off her mind.

A gust of wind kicked up and blew the blanket that was stretched across the cave opening. That brought Echo's mind back to the present. She threw another blanket over her bedroll but couldn't get warm. Her teeth chattered and her body shivered. Then a flash lit up the cave followed by a crack of thunder. The blanket across the cave door blew off on one side. The captain and her brother ran to the cave door and secured the blanket, Dean holding the ladder while the captain tied the blanket to the hooks. Echo sat and watched. She was too cold to move. She glanced over at the girl, who was fast asleep.

The captain came over to where Echo was nestled in her bedroll and blankets. "Strand, are you okay?"

"I think so, Captain. Just cold."

She knelt down and felt Echo's forehead with the palm of her hand. "No fever."

Funny, Echo thought. The captain and I have known each other for almost two years, and I still call her Captain instead of her first name, Dana, and she still addresses me as Strand. But once you get used to calling someone by a certain name, it's hard to change.

The wind was still billowing the blanket at the cave's door, but the blanket stayed secured to the hooks.

The captain was still kneeling at Echo's side when another bolt of thunder cracked. Echo began shivering again.

"Strand, can you stand up?"

"I think so. Why?"

"Come on over to my spot and we'll sit for a while until this storm dies down."

"Okay." Echo stood but almost fell as the blankets and bedroll slowly fell from her body and twisted around her.

The captain put her arm around Echo's waist and walked her over to her spot next to the ledge. Echo became aware that she was light-headed and didn't think she could have walked those few steps on her own. Before sitting down, she scoped the cave. "Where are Amando and Jamey?" Echo asked.

"Dean said they're sleeping in the truck."

"Oh." Echo saw Dean across the way, cleaning up the ashes in the fire pit. It appeared the wind had scattered them when the blanket came loose.

The captain lowered Echo to a sitting position and wrapped a Navajo blanket around both of them. Echo's bedroll and blanket had given her more thickness, but she was warm all of a sudden with the Navajo blanket and the captain's body warmth. She stopped shivering and her head cleared. Still, something about the cave felt eerie. She hadn't noticed it before. Briefly, she wondered if it was something in the stew. She mentioned her strange feeling to the captain. The captain just shook her head slowly. "Something feels different to me too. I don't know the cause though."

They sat there with the blanket wrapped around them for quite some time. Echo noticed the wind had stopped blowing the blanket on the cave entrance. Then she heard the tapping of raindrops outside. At first they were barely audible. Then their intensity increased until they pounded down. Echo glanced at the girl. She still slept.

Soon, the rain lightened up and shortly after that, it stopped. "Wish we had put some containers outside to catch the water," the captain said.

"They might have attracted our pursuers," Echo remarked.

"You're right, Strand. I hadn't thought of that."

Echo smiled then yawned. Her head dropped, and the captain suggested she lie down and use her lap for a pillow.

Echo fell asleep immediately. In her dream she was part of a large family who lived in this same cave, only it was several centuries, or perhaps even millennia, in the past. The people wore leather like historic American Indians and brought food in by donkeys. They were the people on the cave walls. Echo was a boy, perhaps thirteen or fourteen, but she was strong. She hunted coyote and jackrabbits, gutted and skinned them, and cooked them over the fire pit. Her mother lay sick and dying on a blanket—the same blanket the captain had wrapped around the two of them. Its bright colors and geometric patterns especially caught her eye. A medicine woman was hovering over Echo's mother, chanting something in her native language. As Echo removed a cooked rabbit from over the fire and was pulling out its skewer, she heard her mother scream at the top of her lungs.

Echo woke and discovered it was the girl who was screaming. The captain was already making her way down to where the girl lay. She had left Echo's head resting on her silver captain's jacket, its cuff stripes in front of Echo's eyes. Echo's mouth was dry, so she got up to get some water from the truck. She passed the girl and the captain, who was calming her. The men were looking on. Echo wondered if the girl had had a bad dream. Or maybe some local critter had invaded her space. Echo wondered if snakes went inside caves when it rained.

"Dean, would it be okay if I had a cup of water?" Echo asked.

It took a moment for Dean to respond, as he was still watching the girl and the captain. "Oh, uh, sure, Strand. Go ahead."

Echo watched from the back of the truck where the water container was, as the captain coaxed the girl into a sitting position. She glanced around at all of them.

"It's okay, everybody. Just go back to bed."

They all just kept staring, waiting for an explanation. None came. "Go," the captain urged and waved her hand at them.

Reluctantly, they turned away. Echo headed for the facility. When she came out, the captain and the girl were waiting to get in. The girl's face was red and wet from crying. She clearly looked as if she'd been traumatized.

"Captain, tell me there are no snakes in the cave," Echo said.

Her steel blue eyes bore into Echo's. "No snakes, Strand."

Echo went back to bed. For a while she hovered over the ledge and watched the captain calm the girl. Most the time, the captain's hand was on the girl's abdomen, while she spoke to the girl in a soft voice. Finally, Echo turned over and fell into a deep sleep.

When she woke, the cave was filled with daylight. The captain had gathered up her blankets and vacated the spot next to Echo. Echo was sluggish and didn't want to move. To get herself moving, she turned over and stared at the cave wall across the fire pit where Dean had slept. It took a few minutes for her to realize something had changed with the drawings on the wall. Where there had been two donkeys etched in the stone, there was now only one. Maybe her brain wasn't awake yet. She sat up and shook her head. The people in the drawing looked the same, and the coyotes scratched in the rock were also how she remembered them, but yes, now there was only one donkey on the wall. She looked up at the ceiling and there seemed to be fewer hooks than she remembered. I can't deal with this, she thought.

After she'd cleaned up as best as she could, Echo ventured outside. The air was refreshing after the rain the night before, but a lot of muddy puddles remained. She hoped the truck wouldn't get stuck. It shouldn't—it was military grade.

Once they were packed and ready to go, the captain put her arm around Echo's shoulders and whispered into her ear. "I know you are wondering what happened to the girl," she said as they all walked toward the truck that Amando had just driven out of the cave.

Echo nodded. "She had the onset of puberty." That explanation had not occurred to Echo. Poor kid, she thought.

"Is she okay?"

"She's fine now. Her pain has passed."

"Good." Echo wondered if somehow the captain had healed her.

"Another thing, Strand," the captain said aloud. "Her name is Lucy, and she can speak English now."

Chapter 2
Jump Davis

Jump Davis had always been obsessed with money, but never had he been so obsessed with another person, namely, Dana Stewart—Captain Dana Stewart—whom he'd first met when she was merely a spaceplane pilot for TransCom. He had befriended her after her injuries from an accident on the spaceliner. He pretended to uncover some information revealing that TransCom purposely caused the spaceplane accident so their science division could experiment on her brain. However, he had known about the "accident" but didn't tell her.

When Dana officially terminated their relationship, Jump was disappointed but he kept occupied with his corporate ventures on Mars, obtaining as much of the precious ore, uzerium, a natural resource of Mars, as he could.

Not much later, Dana had taken up with her first officer, Coop Wilson. When that happened, something inside Jump had snapped. If he couldn't have Dana, then no one else could either. In a last desperate attempt, Jump confronted her before her long mission to the asteroid belt. He tried to get her to implant a new power supply into her brain, telling her it would give her extra longevity. After she refused, he became livid. He placed it into her hands anyway, hoping she would have a change of heart. By now she had probably discovered the new power supply was no good. Once implanted, it would trigger an explosion in less than twenty-four hours. But now he was glad he hadn't killed her with the new power supply. He had another plan and wanted her alive, at least until he got what he wanted from her.

It had been a very long twelve months waiting for Dana's return, but the spaceplane had brought her and her crew back from Atlantis Space Station a few weeks ago. All along, Jump had planned her entrapment. He would send out a couple of his hired people to capture her. He had pondered giving her an ultimatum—either she stay with him or she die. He knew she would refuse, so he instructed his people to render her unconscious if they must, but not to kill her.

Jump remembered when he'd encountered Dana on the spaceplane as she was ready to take it back to Earth. She was still relatively new with TransCom Spacelines, and he had been a systems analyst for the corporation for a little over a year. She was leaving the lunar base with a plane full of passengers headed toward Los Angeles. She had discovered something wrong with the plane's computer, and Jump was sent on board to check it out. As he stepped into the flight deck, he was struck by Dana's beauty. Actually, "beauty" was an understatement. When she stood up to give him her pilot's seat, her full height unfolded into a regal, commanding stature. Her deep blue eyes bored into his, and Jump was momentarily taken aback. Her copper skin and silky black shoulder-length hair enhanced her looks. Her slim, sinewy body brushed against his slacks as she moved to give him access to the control panel. He had to force himself to focus on the computer problem. His breath caught in his lungs just thinking about her.

A few weeks later, he had gotten up the nerve to ask her to join him at the small lunar café for coffee. She had accepted. Then began their casual relationship and later, more serious. He had looked up her profile and found that she was recently divorced and had one child—a girl—but he acted surprised when she revealed that information to him.

Jump knew the time and date Dana's shuttle was to arrive back from her yearlong mission. Of course, he wasn't allowed on the USSA base. He'd been permanently banned since Coop Wilson reported him to the authorities. It was only because of good lawyers and a lack of solid evidence that he wasn't in prison for attempted murder.

Once Dana moved into her new house off base, it didn't take long for Jump to find her. He wouldn't show his face, of course, but he was able to hack into one of the cloaked aerial drones, common in neighborhoods to keep an eye on intruders. The trick was to alter it so that she could not communicate back to the police if she found out an unauthorized person was watching her. That took some doing, but within a couple of weeks of Dana's move into the house, Jump could keep track of her comings and goings. Unfortunately, he was unable to see inside the house, but what he did know was that Coop Wilson lived there and young Echo Strand had visited several times.

Now Jump was frustrated more than he'd ever been before. Dana had avoided being captured. Jump had chosen a time when he thought Wilson was gone from her house. It was dark outside, just past 8:00 p.m., when his hired man and woman, dressed in black and wearing face masks, snuck up to Dana's window. Jump couldn't believe it—she hadn't even installed a perimeter security alarm. Jump's people had broken the bedroom window and grabbed Dana. But Dana was incredibly strong and proved herself efficient in martial arts. She hit the police button on her comm. Wilson and Echo Strand ran to her rescue, but Jump's people scrambled out the window and got away before the police arrived. At least this is what Dana had reported to the police. Jump had accessed the police files without being traced.

So, Jump Davis had to revise his plans, but before he could try and capture Dana again, she vacated her premises. Evidently, her brother came down from Canada and whisked her away to the Mojave Desert. Jump wasn't sure who else was with them, but he instructed his people to attach an explosive and a tracking device to their vehicle. He could detonate the explosive whenever he wanted. He would choose a time when no one was in the truck, but the explosion would delay Dana's trip enough for his people to capture her. Hopefully, Dana and her brother wouldn't change vehicles before Dana was captured.

Chapter 3
Spike

Echo, the captain, and company rolled into the town of Spike just before noon. Although they had air conditioning in the back of their deuce-and-a-half, it was still over a hundred degrees outside, and Echo felt the heat seeping through. Plus, all of them needed showers desperately, especially young Lucy who'd been on her own for days. Dean sat up front with Amando, who did most the driving, though occasionally they switched off. Jamey, Lucy, the captain, and Echo sat or lay on their piles of bedrolls and blankets in the back.

Jamey had gotten Lucy to open up about her past. He was sixteen and she a mere twelve years of age, but she took a liking to him from the start. They spoke to each other in Spanish, though they could both speak and understand English. Spanish was just more natural for them. Plus, Echo thought Lucy had a small crush on Jamey. He was handsome with his lanky body, smooth skin, and jet-black hair. His eyes were a deep brown and seemed to express laughter, but showed an underlying sadness. Echo didn't know his story, but she probably would before this trip was over.

If Lucy were telling the truth, and Echo wasn't at all convinced, then she had hidden from the border patrol while she and her mother and father were crossing from Mexico into California. Her parents had gotten caught, but Lucy was too afraid of being shot. She didn't know what these border patrol would do to illegal immigrants. But if that were so, how had she ended up in the California desert? After this clandestine trip, the captain and Dean would probably try and return her to her parents in Mexico. Lucy had hidden behind a scrubby tree several hundred meters from the capture of her parents. The patrol people had guns, and she was afraid of being shot. She didn't know if her parents would be jailed or sent back to Mexico or shot. But she had spent the little money she had on food and was left to hang out at a convenience store in the small town where Dean had found her.

"Quite a story," the captain whispered in Echo's ear when the girl wasn't looking.

"I want to believe her," Echo said. "At any rate, she's with us now." The truth was that Echo thought she was probably a runaway. Maybe the mother or father was abusive. It was as if Echo had gained a sixth sense about the situation. It was only her logical mind that doubted. She knew that homeless kids often lied.

The town of Spike lived up to its name. It was dressed up as a nineteenth century western town, only the railroad had been removed—most of it anyway. A steam locomotive engine with a freight car and caboose made a permanent fixture behind the town's saloon and rested on just enough railroad track to support it. The rest of the track had been ripped up and recycled as scrap metal. The ties were a valuable source of wood, and the spikes were used for a variety of items from everything from table legs and fence posts to the town's gigantic analog clock hoisted high above the city hall. Not only was the town dusty like the old cowboy towns of the 1800s, it sported a museum-like quality, old buggies, plows, horse hitching posts, and even a working blacksmith and a livery stable, which sold horse rides.

Dean and Echo walked into the hotel's lobby and asked for two rooms with three beds each. The clerk, dressed in a nineteenth century suit, tie, and vest, gave each of them a suspicious look, then asked for a credit card.

"I thought credit cards were not in use anymore," Echo said. "You know, since the new president?"

The clerk looked puzzled. "I haven't heard anything about that."

I must have missed something the year I was gone on the spaceship, Echo thought. But she had kept up with the newsfeeds. Hmm. Must've missed that one.

"We only have cash," Dean said. He laid out several large bills.

The clerk was apprehensive. "Don't know. The boss says we have to take a credit card. If one of your party had a credit card for collateral, that would do.

"Just a minute," Dean said to the clerk then pulled Echo aside. "Echo, go find Dana and tell her I need a two-ounce bar of uzerium."

Echo's eyes popped open. She had been unaware Dean had brought any of the precious ore along on the trip. He'd been thinking ahead though, like maybe he might have to bribe someone to get out of a tricky situation. She ran outside where Amando was sitting in the truck.

In his broken English he indicated that the captain had gone into town with the girl.

"Well, I need a two-ounce bar of uzerium. Dean needs it." Amando frowned. "U-ZER-I-UM," Echo said. She held up two fingers to indicate two ounces.

Amando held up a finger, then got out of the cab of the truck indicating he wanted her to wait right there.

Echo couldn't see exactly where he went, but it looked as if he crawled under the truck. Moments later he came back with a small felt bag and handed it to her. She peeked inside. Inside was a two by six-centimeter brass colored polished bar of compressed uzerium. She ran her fingers over its silky surface.

Amando pointed inside the bag. "Stay in bag."

"I'll keep it out of sight," Echo said. She dashed back to the hotel and found Dean where she'd left him. She slipped the bag containing the bar into his hands.

"Will this suffice for payment?" Dean asked the hotel clerk.

The clerk's eyes popped out. "Uh yes, of course," he said.

Echo could tell by the look on his face that he wanted to ask where the uzerium came from and if Dean had more. But the clerk just gave them their room keys and directed them to their rooms. There was no bellhop, which Echo found unusual, but that got them out of tipping.

The men's hotel room adjoined the women's with a locking door between rooms. Each room had two double beds, so someone would have to double up in a bed or sleep on the floor. Echo hoped she would get a bed to herself. She liked the privacy of sleeping alone, even living with her partner, Sanders, at home or on the spaceship.

Echo plopped her belongings down on one of the beds and went to the window. The room had a good view of the main street outside. Suddenly, she felt the need to find the captain. For some reason, she felt the captain was in danger and should be out of sight from the public. Echo wandered in and out of stores in the one-street business district but could not find the captain and Lucy. She first checked the grocery store across from the hotel. Then she went into a variety store that sold souvenirs, clothing, and junk food. While there, she bought herself a can of cola. Then she ducked into a second-hand clothing store, and next, a hardware store. Unable to locate the captain, she crossed the street and headed back to the hotel.

On the way back to the hotel, Echo stopped by city hall just to check it out. In the lobby were two small screens with rotating "wanted" posters. She thought they were phony, just put on for the western theme of the town. She stood and watched the alternating displays to see if they showed any familiar faces. Some of the pictures were of outlaws long gone, like Jesse James. Those were on one of the screens. On the other screen were people who wore modern clothing and hairstyles. She was about to leave when a picture of the captain flashed on the screen. Echo shook her head but the picture remained. She told the display to stop and asked for more information. The picture showed the captain from the chest up, but Echo could tell she was wearing her USSA captain's uniform, silver jacket with captain's pips on the collar. Echo thought it looked like an old picture, but the captain hadn't aged much since her brain implant shortly after resigning with TransCom. Echo read the details: WANTED BY THE FBI FOR MURDER. PLEASE CONTACT THIS COMM NUMBER IF YOU HAVE SEEN THIS PERSON. $100,000 REWARD IN U.S. CURRENCY.

Echo's heart pounded. She couldn't believe the captain murdered anyone. If anything, she was framed or if she had killed someone, it would have been in self-defense. At any rate, she couldn't have been hired by USSA had she committed any crime.

As she was entering the hotel, Echo ran into the captain and Lucy. "I have to talk to you," Echo said anxiously.

The captain extended her arms and put her hands on Echo's shoulders. "Calm down," she said. "You look like you've just seen a ghost."

Echo glanced at Lucy. The captain handed Lucy a bill and asked her to go get some hot chocolate. Lucy dropped her shopping bags and ran off to the concession area. Echo picked up the bags, the captain picked up hers, and they walked over to some soft chairs and sat down.

"Now, what is it, Strand?"

Echo described the FBI wanted photo to her and suggested she don a disguise as soon as possible.

"I want to see this. Sounds like one of Jump Davis' tricks."

"That's what I thought," Echo said.

None of the group had brought their comms with them, as electronic equipment could be traced. Echo and the captain went over to a public comm booth in the lobby and looked up the FBI wanted pictures. The captain gasped when she saw her picture. The information said she had sought out and gunned down Jump Davis in cold blood. "So, Davis wants me to think he's dead as well. This is a big crock."

For a rare moment, Echo saw the captain angered. All the time she'd known her, she had pretty much kept her cool.

"Maybe you could cut your hair—even color it. And get your eyes colored," Echo said. But Echo didn't like the idea of the captain disguising those unique blue eyes.

The captain turned toward Echo and gave her one of her icy, penetrating stares. For a few seconds she said nothing, then, "I'll do no such thing. That psychopath isn't going to force me to change my looks. He's already forced me from my home."

Echo looked at her with apprehension. "I'm going to bleach my hair, just in case I'm recognizable too. You need to do something."

"All right, I'll cut my hair and get some sunglasses." She removed her silver USSA jacket. "And wear a different jacket."

Echo rubbed her wrist where she still retained her barely visible barcode. "We need to change your ID," Echo said.

"I don't know anyone who can do that," said the captain.

"I could give it a try, but I suggest we get your disguise in place and talk to the others first."

"Lucy," the captain said, as if she'd forgotten about the girl.

They found Lucy sitting on a bar stool in a small café built into the hotel. She was sipping on a hot chocolate from a porcelain mug. She was still wearing her rags and needed a bath desperately.

The captain took her hand. "C'mon honey, let's get you cleaned up and into some of those new clothes."

"But I haven't finished," Lucy said. She must have noticed the captain's anxiety. "What's wrong?"

"Nothing, honey," the captain lied. "I'm just eager to get a shower and change of clothes. Doesn't that sound good?"

"I'll have them put your hot chocolate in a to-go cup," Echo said.

Lucy seemed to accept that and hopped off the barstool. As soon as the to-go cup arrived, the three of them ascended the stairs to their room.

Echo dashed out to the variety store and picked up a hair coloring kit. The instructions said it would take an hour for the entire process of turning her hair blonde. Any less time, her hair could turn orange. By the time she was back, the captain and Lucy had taken their showers and changed.

When Echo had finished with her hair (which didn't look bad, she had to admit) and her shower, she went downstairs to use the public computers. She had no problem finding the captain's ID but couldn't alter it, not even her address. There were too many firewalls. They'd have to settle for leaving her identity as it was for now. Echo just hoped she wasn't asked for her ID before they got all this business straightened out. But she was worried about the Canadian border.

Echo stepped outside to check on the truck, which was parked in a fenced lot in back of the hotel. She wondered if the uzerium box had been taken inside. And then a premonition struck her—they should take everything inside. She didn't know why, but it was such a strong gut feeling that she ran back inside the hotel and up the stairs.

The captain's shoulder length hair was still damp, and she was drying it with a towel. "Oh, Strand, how are you at cutting hair?"

"Uh, I don't know—I've only trimmed my own from time to time."

"Well, it should be easier for you to do someone else's."

"Captain, before we get to that, I think we need to get everything out of the truck. Now."

She frowned at Echo. "You know, we've got a lot of stuff in that truck. Why do you want us to bring everything in, Strand? It's in a secure lot."

Echo took a deep breath. "I don't really know—I just have a strong feeling about it."

The captain studied Echo for a moment. Then she walked over to the adjoining door and knocked on it. "Dean, open up."

Echo stayed in the room with Lucy, who was playing with some string beads she had laid out on the bed. She was dressed in a new pair of girls' blue Levis and a pink T-shirt with white daisies on it, and she wore white walking shoes. Her dark hair was long and silky and almost dry from having been in the shower. She looked like a regular kid. Echo stuck her hands into her pockets and felt the loose change and bills. She still didn't trust the kid—often orphans and homeless kids would steal from people. However, Echo didn't get a strong feeling about Lucy one way or another.

Echo plopped down on the bed next to her and tried to take an interest in what she was doing, but actually, Echo was listening to the conversation between the captain and her brother.

"Dean, it wouldn't hurt to follow Strand's gut feeling about this."

"But we've got *so* much stuff in that truck—piles of blankets, bedrolls, flares, laser pistols, not to mention our water containers. What's it gonna look like hauling all that stuff inside the hotel? Dragging it through the lobby?"

"Well, I hope you've at least brought in the uzerium box."

A brief silence followed. "I'll get it right now," Dean said. "But all that other stuff—."

The captain's voice lowered in volume but Echo could still hear her. "Strand's developed a sort of sixth sense, I believe. I think we should pay attention to it."

Another brief silence followed. Then a sigh. "All right, Dana, but I think it's a waste of time."

The captain stayed with Lucy while Echo helped Dean, Amando, and Jamey bring in all their goods from the truck. They didn't speak to Echo or to one another as they worked. Echo felt guilty for suggesting they transfer stuff from the truck into the hotel, but she was also relieved they were doing it. They wrapped the guns in blankets and all they got were a few curious stares as they traipsed through the hotel lobby five or six times.

Lucy was curled up on the bed clutching her stomach when Echo returned to their room. The captain was in the facility with the door closed.

"What's wrong, kid?" Echo asked Lucy.

"It hurts," she squeaked out.

Cramps, Echo thought. "You want some analgesic?"

She nodded.

Echo pawed through the first aid kit, glad she had brought it inside from the truck. Finally, she found a bottle of pills that said to take with food. They didn't have any food in the hotel room. Echo had decided to leave the protein bars in the truck—no big loss if someone stole those.

"Be right back," Echo said and ran downstairs to grab a bag of chips out of the food vending machine. It still seemed odd to her to insert coins into a machine. Before the new president, before the breakup of the monopolies, people had only to wave their wristcodes over a sensor to purchase anything from a transit fare to an ice cream cone. Using currency was a novelty but it was also downright inconvenient.

Echo zoomed into the hotel room to find the captain bent over Lucy with her hands hovering above the girl's abdomen. The first thing Echo noticed though was the captain's short hair. She'd evidently cropped it herself. Lucy was on her back with knees bent and her eyes closed. Her face was relaxed. Echo sensed she shouldn't say anything until this healing session, or whatever the captain was doing, was finished. She set the bag of chips on the chest of drawers, sat in a chair, and watched with curiosity. After about fifteen minutes, the girl appeared to be asleep, and the captain covered her gently with a blanket.

The captain withdrew from the bed and walked over to Echo. "She should be okay for a while."

"How did you know what to do?"

The captain shook her head. "That's the thing. I don't know."

"Something really spooky is happening," Echo said, trying to sound like she was joking, but she really meant it.

"Something is a little off," the captain said. "But I can't tell you what."

"I sensed that too." She silently wondered if the captain would be able to heal a cut or a scratch.

That afternoon, Jamey, Lucy, and Echo set out for a walk through town. Echo left Jamey and Lucy at a local park while she found a used clothing store to buy herself another set of clothing as well as some men's clothing for the captain's disguise. Since Spike was a tourist type western town, it wasn't difficult to find a cowboy hat. Echo purchased a nice white one for the captain, who had given her adequate currency for both of them. The captain already had sunglasses, so Echo didn't need to buy those. As for western boots, the captain would have to try those on herself.

Jamey and Lucy were swinging on the swings when Echo dropped back by the park to pick them up. They didn't want to leave, but Echo felt they shouldn't be out any longer, especially as it was approaching sunset. After some coaxing, she finally persuaded them to come back to the hotel for dinner. Echo was tired, so they all jumped on a trolley car and rode the six or seven blocks back.

The group ate in the men's hotel room, as the women's was covered with blankets and other supplies from the truck. Dean, being against bringing all the stuff in from the truck in the first place, had decided the women's room should accommodate it all—except for the box of uzerium—he kept guard over that. The food tasted good—cheeseburgers, country fries, salad, milk, and soda.

Jamey and Lucy wanted to eat in the restaurant, but the captain wanted all of them together so she could tell everyone about the FBI alert out for her. She explained that Jump Davis probably initiated a lie about her and hacked into the FBI site.

"Wow," Jamey said.

"This information is strictly hush-hush," Dean told him.

"Of course," said Jamey, and Lucy nodded. She still didn't talk very much.

Echo spoke up. "Has anyone noticed anything unusual about themselves since we left the cave?"

Everyone was silent for a moment, looking around at one another. Then Jamey spoke up. "Lucy didn't know English before the cave."

"Yes, I know," said the captain.

"What about Amando?" Echo asked. "Can he speak English now?"

Jamey asked him in Spanish, and Amando shook his head. "Like before, not much."

"Dean?" the captain asked. "Anything unusual going on with you?"

"Not that I know of," Dean said. "But I think we should get out of town as soon as possible before Dana is identified. The middle of the night would be ideal, but we have to load up the truck, so we'll have to make it just after dawn." He glared at Echo, not harshly, but just enough to let her know he was still unhappy about her instinct to unload the truck.

"Better safe than sorry," Echo told him without malice.

"I'm going to disguise myself as a man," the captain said. "Strand has already picked up my clothing. I just need some boots."

"Amando can remove your identity wristcode," Jamey said.

Before the captain could answer, Dean spoke up. He had gotten his wristcode removed a long time ago. "That might help for a while, but there are always DNA tests and retinal scans. She'd have to get a full workup in the hospital."

"Maybe in Canada when she gets her brain implant removed," Echo suggested.

The captain wiped her mouth with her napkin and stood up. "Hold on, everyone. I'm not getting anything done except a change of clothes. I wasn't even going to do that, but I reconsidered."

"And your haircut," Dean said. He examined her hair. "You could do with a little evening up," he suggested.

"Amando's good at cutting hair," Jamey said. He said something to Amando in Spanish making a hair clipping motion with his fingers pointing to the captain."

Amando nodded.

It took Echo a long time to go to sleep even though she got a double bed to herself. Lucy piled a big stack of blankets on the floor, covered them with a bedroll, and crawled inside, as happy as Echo had ever seen her.

It seemed as if Echo had only slept a couple of hours when she was awakened by what sounded like a loud explosion. She sat up abruptly. Daylight was just starting to filter through the old-fashioned flowery curtains. She jumped up and parted the drapes, clad only in her pajama bottoms and T-shirt. She saw nothing. The sound seemed to have come from the other side of the hotel.

The captain had already donned her "new" clothing that Echo had purchased at the second-hand store, slipped on her western boots she'd acquired the night before after dinner, and was putting on her hat. Echo got a glimpse of her refined haircut, touched up by Amando's expertise, before she slipped the hat onto her head.

"Wait for me," Echo said. But the captain was out the door without a word. Echo scurried to get dressed and helped Lucy up. "Stay here," Echo told her in the sternest voice she could muster.

The truck was completely blown to bits, and much of the debris landed on other vehicles in the parking lot. The hotel manager and other staff were gathering, as well as people from other parts of town. Dean arrived on the scene within moments. The captain was ordering people to stand back, taking charge of the situation.

Once the initial shock was over, Dean confronted Echo. "How did you know?" His voice was accusatory.

"I didn't," Echo said.

"You told us to bring our things inside. You must have known the truck was in danger."

The captain heard their interchange and came over to them. "What's going on here?"

"How did she know the truck was going to blow up?" Dean said to the captain. "She had us take stuff out of the truck, Dana. She *had* to know *some*thing."

The captain took her brother aside, but Echo could still hear what they said.

"You should be thanking her, Dean. We would have lost all our supplies including the uzerium."

"I was going to bring that in," he said.

"Just calm down. We've got a bigger problem on our hands. We're going to need new transportation."

Echo didn't hear what else they said because Dean took the captain farther away from her. Echo could already hear the sirens in the distance, coming closer to the scene. Then all of a sudden, the captain ran toward Echo and grabbed her arm.

"Go get Lucy and a few of our belongings and meet me in the alley behind the bus station."

"But what are we doing?"

"Just do as I ask—I'll explain later." She gave Echo's back a gentle shove then lost herself in the gathering crowd.

Lucy was reluctant to leave, as she was busy playing an interactive video game Dean had rented from the hotel. Echo had to help her off with the gear, a lightweight body suit that was too large on her. She was also cranky, probably from awakening too early.

"Leave me alone," she cried like a spoiled child, not a grateful child who'd been rescued from the California desert, cleaned and fed and given new clothing. How do parents put up with this behavior, Echo wondered?

"The captain is waiting for us."

"So?"

Echo finally had to threaten her. "Do you want to go to jail?"

She gave Echo a pout before answering. "No."

"Well our truck blew up and we're all going to be taken to the police station for questioning if we don't make ourselves scarce. Is that what you want?"

Another pause. "No."

"Then grab your jacket and new clothes, stuff them in a bag, and let's go!"

All this time Echo was gathering up her things as well as the captain's clothes that needed laundering. She also snatched up the captain's sneakers—she'd soon get tired of those cowboy boots. I hope she has some money, Echo thought, or better yet, some bars of uzerium in case more places wanted credit cards for collateral. Sure would be nice to have some electronics of our own. Maybe down the road.

With a heavy pack on Echo's back and Lucy carrying a small sports bag, the two of them climbed out the window and onto the fire escape. The stairs stopped at about two meters from the ground, a paved alley speckled with green dumpsters. They threw their bags onto the ground and jumped onto a dumpster (fortunately the lid was closed) a little off to their right. Echo jumped down to street level first, then she helped Lucy, who looked both excited and scared.

Echo hefted the backpack onto her back with a grunt, and Lucy picked up her bag. Echo took her free hand and they ran down the alley until they hit a cross street. Echo was unsure exactly where the bus station was, but she was pretty sure they were headed in the right direction. Her main concern was to stay out of sight.

After four blocks, the alleys stopped. Echo didn't know whether to go right or left, but after a few seconds of having her eyes shut, her newly acquired intuition kicked in, and she knew going left was the proper direction. This took them up to Main Street, which they crossed as quickly as possible over to State Route 20, and voilà, there was the bus depot.

The sun was fully up now, and Echo felt visible, exposed. Of course no one was after her, but she'd been seen with the captain, who they *were* after. Echo believed her that Jump Davis had hacked into the FBI computers and accused her of killing him. He must really hate her, Echo thought.

At first, Echo couldn't find the captain. Her heart raced. Then Lucy tugged on her arm and pointed. The captain was emerging from the men's room. Echo giggled. She couldn't help it. The captain still wore her western boots and hat with her jeans and western shirt. She was probably hiding in there until the time she thought Echo and Lucy would show up. Good timing, Echo thought.

"Let's go to Gate A," the captain said. "I've already got our tickets."

Echo noticed the captain's jacket pockets were weighted down and hoped they were filled with uzerium. "Where are we going?" Echo asked.

"Reno."

Chapter 4
Reno

"I didn't know the truck was going to blow up," Echo told the captain once they were traveling on the road to Reno."

"I believe you," she said. "Dean'll come around. He just needs time."

Echo was sitting next to the window and gazed out at the highway. Every so often the bus hit a crack in the cement, which gave them a jolt. She wondered why the invisible energy current wasn't moving them along. They were propelled solely by the bus' own power sources—electricity and hydrogen fuel. The economy must have taken a nosedive while we were gone on our yearlong mission to the asteroid belt, Echo thought. Not that it was in great shape when they left, but the highways were still operational.

Something about this whole experience was out of joint. Echo wondered how she knew to bring their supplies in from the truck. She certainly hadn't had a vision of the truck blowing up. She decided to try something and hoped the captain wouldn't be upset about it, but if she was, oh well.

Echo took her pocketknife out of her jacket and held out her forearm. Her back was turned to the captain so she couldn't see what Echo was doing. She held her bandana ready on her lap as she made a small incision in her arm. Ouch. She didn't utter anything out loud, but her body jerked enough for the captain to notice. Blood oozed, out of her arm, and she blotted it with her bandana while folding her knife back up.

"What's going on?" the captain asked.

"I cut myself." Echo removed the bloodstained bandana from her arm. "I want you to put your hand over my wound." Echo covered it with the bandana again so the captain wouldn't have to touch her blood. The captain hesitated. "Please."

The captain put her palm over Echo's bandana-covered wound and curled her fingers around Echo's arm. She held her hand there for about thirty seconds, eyeing Echo with a hint of disapproval.

"Okay, you can let go," Echo said. Echo removed the bandana. Her cut had turned to a thin healed scab.

"I don't know how that happened," the captain said. "But I do know I've had some kind of healing ability since the cave."

"Yes, when I had the chills, you put your arm around me and they went away. It happened right after the electrical storm."

"Hold out your arm again, this time without the bandana."

Echo did as she was told, and the captain put her hand over the scab. This time she closed her eyes, and for the first time since Echo had known her, she saw faint age lines on the captain's face. She wasn't supposed to age—not for a long time—not with that implant in her brain. She was beginning to look older than her forty-four years. The captain removed her hand after a few seconds, and Echo's scab was gone—replaced by a thin white scar. After a few minutes, the scar disappeared. Echo didn't know what to say except to thank her.

They rode along in silence for a long time, Lucy sitting behind Echo and the captain, playing with the miniature video game the captain had bought her in Spike. Echo thought about the truck and wondered who had planted the explosive devices that blew it up. Even with her enhanced intuition, she had no idea. She thought about meeting up with Dean, Jamey, and Amando, and wondered what kind of vehicle they had acquired.

They passed a sign that read, Altitude 1258 Meters. Echo was used to sea level, but the altitude climb was gradual, so she didn't notice too much until she stood up and became light-headed. When she returned from the facility, the captain told her they were almost there. Up until then, Echo hadn't asked her what they were going to do once they arrived at the Reno bus depot. She would let the captain take the lead. After all, Dean had spoken with her before they left Spike, and Echo assumed they had a plan.

The Reno bus depot was large and modern with transparent computer screens filling the walls and ceiling, displays changing every few seconds.

"Wait here with Lucy," the captain ordered. Echo watched as she headed for a public comm booth and closed the door.

"I'm hungry," Lucy told Echo.

"I'm sure we'll get something to eat soon," Echo reassured her.

After a few minutes the captain emerged from the booth and headed their way. She was still dressed as a man but had removed the large hat. "Dean and the others will meet us at the Best Bet Diner. It's only a few blocks away."

While they were waiting for their order, the six of them squished into a booth, and Dean passed out some small comms to each of them. Echo picked hers up. It looked peculiar, not like the comms she remembered from a year ago before the space mission. These were tiny fold-up jobs with keypads that even Echo's small fingers had a hard time pushing. Echo didn't make any comments; she just decided to let Dean speak.

"Make sure you don't use them to contact anyone but each other," he said. "I've got a friend who lives in a modular home out in the woods near the mountains, just north of here. He's agreed to make us some plastic IDs and credit cards. I acquired a used van in Spike. It's in the underground parking garage near here. We can all ride together but should meet at the vehicle separately, so as not to bring any attention to our group."

Echo was suddenly struck with a very strange feeling. Credit cards? Plastic IDs? Funny looking comms? She looked at each person at the booth. Did Dean look older? Didn't he have a few more lines in his face and graying at the temples than a couple of days ago? Amando's head was buried in the electronic menu inset into the table. He didn't look any worse for wear but then again, Echo hadn't paid much attention to him. Jamey still looked as young as ever except tired in the face. Then Echo turned to Lucy, who was sitting beside her. She looked a little worn as well. Echo glanced over at the captain, two seats away. A stabbing shock hit her heart. She saw a few strands of gray in her now short-cropped hair in addition to the faint lines she'd seen on her face when they were riding on the bus.

Echo didn't want to mention anything to the others, but she had a definite sense that they'd transported into another dimension, alternate timeline, or parallel universe. Her logical mind said no, that's only science fiction. But her newly acquired heightened intuition gave her a big yes.

The home of Roy Rickerson looked as though it were at least a century old. Its outside light blue-gray wood paneling was patched in a number of places with pieces of corrugated steel, many of them with rusty spots. The roof was A-shaped and looked like crumbling and tattered composition shingle with various tar patched spots. The walkway up to the door was littered with rocks and branches, as was the small yard.

Dean knocked on the front door, the rest of them trailing behind. After at least a minute of waiting, the door opened and a friendly bearded face appeared. Roy was taller than any of them, and wider as well, but not obese. He had a Santa Claus-shaped beard of red and gray and a fuzzy head full of hair—no balding that Echo could see. They all stepped into the house, Echo being the last.

"Dean-o, what kind of trouble have you gotten yourself into this time?" Roy asked with a friendly air. Roy examined Dean for a moment. "You look a little green around the gills my friend." Roy stepped aside so Dean and the rest of the group could enter his home. "Oh, excuse me." Roy swept stacks of books, hand-held computers, and papers from several chairs and a couch onto the floor. "Please, sit down everyone." Echo found herself a small stool, removed a bag of chips, and sat down.

Echo glanced around the room. She eyed a large orange cat perched on a ragged cat condo, staring at everyone intensely. Roy had at least ten computer screens in various places and one central control with a big chair for himself at a console in the midst of them. There was also large, heavy machinery in three areas of the room. Echo detected a faint smell of corn chips, marijuana, and cat pee. She hoped they could get out of this place soon because the room was stuffy and the wood stove was cranking out a lot of heat.

The first task was for Roy to take all their pictures. He had an old-fashioned digital camera without holo capabilities. The captain got three IDs—one of her real identity in case for some reason she was exonerated for her supposed crime. And two other phony names—Pricilla Hardwick and Donella Dravis. Echo was instructed to carry the IDs the captain would not be using at one time or another. Then another thought struck Echo—perhaps the Captain Stewart of this timeline *had* killed Jump Davis. Echo selfishly and guiltily thought to herself that she could be seen as an accessory—they all could. Too late now. She was loyal to this captain anyway. As for the other captain—the wanted one—she wasn't so sure. Maybe they could find someone to send them back to their own timeline. She'd have to convince the others first. She didn't want to admit to being afraid of Dean, but he'd have to be convinced if they were to find a scientist to transport them back to their own timeline. Dean seemed to have clandestine connections that might help. Echo just didn't like him snapping at her like he had when the truck blew up. She'd tell the captain and let her talk to him.

"What about removing our wristcodes?" Echo asked Roy. Echo held out her arm. "It would be just for me and the captain, er, Dana, here."

Roy was a friendly guy, but he gave Echo a puzzled look. "Wristcodes?"

"Never mind," Echo said.

Pretty soon their IDs and credit cards started spitting out of one of the big machines. Dean walked over to examine them, turning each one over in his hands, taking his time reading each card. He then set them down and went to his bag, pulled out three small bars of uzerium, and set them on the table. Then he and Roy shook hands. Roy's face beamed as he held the uzerium, massaging it in his hands.

Dean passed out the cards. Each card was about eight centimeters long by five centimeters wide with a magnetic strip on the back. Echo had heard these types of cards were used in the twenty-first century, but she'd never actually seen any. She wondered then if they might have traveled back in time, but immediately disregarded that idea. After all, Roy Rickerson knew Dean. If they'd gone back a hundred years or so, Roy would not have been born yet. But just to make sure, Echo glanced around the room looking for a calendar.

"May I get a drink of water?" Echo asked Roy. She interrupted him while he was chatting with Amando in Spanish, but he didn't seem to mind. Roy was perched on the arm of his couch with one foot propped on a folding chair. He immediately stood up and clapped his hands.

"Oh, I'm sorry, dear. I didn't offer anyone anything to drink. Yes, yes, there is water, beer, and soda in the fridge. Please, help yourselves."

"Thanks," Echo told him. She wound around all the furniture and equipment and made her way to the kitchen, which was just as cluttered, with a too big table piled with various and sundry items and four chairs scattered here and there. The refrigerator was packed. Roy probably shopped by the month, stocking up because he was out in the woods. Echo dug around and found a can of cola. She popped it open and drenched her dry mouth in its delicious sweet carbonation. She closed the door and noticed among the digital pictures covering the refrigerator door, a small calendar, month October, year 2129. Of course it was possible that Roy had not bothered changing the calendar, but if the correct year was posted, the months should change automatically. But who knew in this world of plastic IDs and credit cards? Their new comms didn't show the date, but according to Echo's memory of when they left Los Angeles, it should be October 9, 2129.

"Hey, anyone want pizza?" Roy asked.

Jamey stepped up to the refrigerator, followed by Lucy, and Echo moved aside. He took out a soda for himself and one for Lucy.

"Not if we have to have it delivered," the captain said. "We don't want any attention drawn to us, if you know what I mean."

Roy frowned and put his finger to his forehead. "Think I got a couple of frozen ones out in the back room. Won't be as good as a freshly delivered one, but they'll be passable, especially if you're hungry."

Echo was hungry. Her stomach was rumbling. She hadn't eaten that much at the diner and it had been several hours. She eyed the captain and gave her a nod.

"Sounds good, Roy. Much appreciated," the captain told him.

"My pleasure."

Roy picked up his uzerium bars and took them into another room. A few minutes later he came out with two large frozen pizzas in his arms. Pretty soon a pizza aroma was added to the existing smells in the house. Echo wondered if Roy was going to bring out his marijuana to share, but no such luck. The pizzas were good enough. Echo didn't need her appetite to increase anymore than it was already. The pepperoni was a little tough but still flavorful, and the mixture of cheese toppings seemed to blend well. The other toppings were tasteless little lumps of odd-shaped and colored pieces and bits. The crust was nice and crisp—just how she liked it.

When they were finished, Dean thanked Roy, and they all filed out the door and into the van. Echo kept trying to figure out a way to get the captain alone so she could run her alternate universe theory by her, but the opportunity just didn't come.

Roy instructed them how to get to the main highway that would take them north and eventually into Canada. Once they were out of the woods, the vehicle seemed to be moving along smoothly on its rubber tires across the better-than-average maintained road. Echo was sacked out in the back of the van among the blankets with Jamey and Lucy, who were tossing a large rubber ball back and forth. Echo had eaten too much, and the cola she'd consumed wasn't helping her stay awake. The captain was in the front seat with Dean and Amando, examining the GPS maps. Echo was just dozing off when she saw a blinding light filter through from the front seat. Then she heard a loud chopping sound coming from outside. "Hold it right there," a disembodied voice announced from somewhere above them.

"Get out of here fast, Amando," Dean said.

Amando swerved to the left, barely missing something coming from the opposite direction. Echo rolled across the back of the van but sat up as soon as possible.

"What's going on?" Echo asked.

"They've found us," Jamey said calmly.

"How?"

"Don't know."

Amando kept swerving, trying to evade the loud air machine. Finally, they ended up off the freeway over an embankment. The back of the van had no side windows, but out the back Echo could see a pod-shaped aircraft with a propeller blade on top approach closer to them. Then she felt and heard a loud thump on the top of their van.

"What was that?" Lucy said.

"Feels like a magnet," said Dean.

"What kind of strange world are we in anyway?" said Lucy. She'd noticed it too.

Chapter 5
Separation Anxiety

In the world Echo knew there were hovercraft—antigrav pods that needed no propellers. This type of aircraft had gone out in the mid-twenty-first century.

"Quick, everyone jump out!" Dean yelled. They had to climb over one another, but eventually Jamey, Lucy, the captain, and Echo emerged from the van's back doors, and Dean and Amando tumbled out the driver's door. Amando had run the van off the freeway into a wooded area. The aircraft was still hovering but had released the cable the magnet was attached to. It couldn't get too close to the ground, as the propeller would get entangled in the nearby trees.

"Stop right there," came a male voice that sounded as if it were coming from a megaphone. They kept running.

Echo looked behind herself. It was dark outside, but the aircraft shined a beam down on them, following their every movement. Echo kept zigging and zagging trying to avoid the beam. The captain was ahead of her, stumbling through the brush, staying low. A sudden impulse caused Echo to swap the captain's ID for one of the fake ones. Then a single figure emerged from the craft on a cable, lowering her—or himself to the ground. A net was cast and the captain was caught in it. The rest of the group remained free. The cable pulled the captain up in the net, capturing her like a trapped animal.

"Get out of here," the captain yelled to them. But Echo couldn't imagine not going after her.

The craft propelled itself away with the captain inside. It wasn't long until it was out of sight, and the whirly chop of the blades faded into the night.

Echo's heart was screaming inside. They had to find the captain. But Echo was paralyzed; she couldn't move, couldn't think. Her numbness was interrupted by Dean's voice.

"C'mon Strand, let's go get the van. It took a moment for Echo's body to snap into action. She looked around. Dean was now shining a light throughout the wooded area, and Echo was able to account for Jamey, Lucy, and Amando.

Breathlessly, they all arrived a few minutes later at their van, tilted slightly to the side, with a giant magnet attached to its top.

Together, all of them managed to tip the vehicle upright, not an easy task with the heavy magnet on top. The wheels were still intact and the frame was not bent. They still had their supplies. Evidently, the people from the aircraft only wanted the captain.

"Let's go after her," Echo said anxiously.

"We'd never be able to find her tonight," Dean told Echo. He seemed resigned to the fact. Echo wished she could accept that, but she had to force herself to.

"We'll track her with our comms. She's already sent a signal."

Echo had forgotten about their comms. She felt slightly better but still had a wrenching feeling in her gut. It was overpowering her intuition, and she couldn't think clearly. Plus, she'd been awake all night worrying. When they were on the ship, they couldn't lose one another. It was impossible unless some of them took off in a shuttle to an asteroid or went outside the ship to do repairs. Still, they knew where one another were all the time. But this situation was gut wrenching. They were even lost in an alternate universe. She'd have to talk to Dean about that, eventually.

They stayed hidden in the woods, sleeping in the van, until daylight. Then they went back to Roy's to regroup and make a plan. He welcomed them but was clearly surprised to see them again.

Dean gave Roy another bar of uzerium, and Roy treated them to bacon, eggs, and pancakes. Echo was clearly hungrier than she'd realized, and she gobbled up two large pancakes and even tried some of Roy's coffee, which wasn't bad. Her stomach had settled down enough to get her breakfast down, but soon afterward, her guts tied up in a big knot. She excused herself from the table and sat in a chair. The others continued yakking away, while Echo unconsciously grabbed her abdomen and closed her eyes.

A few minutes later, Dean was standing over her, looking into her eyes. "You feel okay, Strand?"

"Not really," she admitted.

"Just a minute," Dean said and whispered something to Roy. They both came back to her. "Strand, Roy has something that might help you relax."

"What?"

"C'mon back to my workroom," Roy said. To Echo, the entire house looked like a workroom.

The three of them entered one of the back bedrooms, which was decked out with historical war memorabilia. Three-D pictures of military garb all the way back to the American Civil War lined the walls. The ceiling displayed several flags from European to South American to African to Asian countries. A part of one wall had different versions of American flags from the thirteen colonies to the present. Echo thought the flag with the most stars was from the present until she counted only fifty stars on it. In her universe, there were fifty-six stars on the flag. A single bed was tucked into the corner with olive drab wool blankets on top. Dioramas made from fish tanks, stacked three high, lined another wall.

"Sit," Roy told Echo as he gestured to the bed. Echo sat down while Dean and Roy each took a chair.

"Strand," Dean said. "Have you ever smoked marijuana?"

The question took her by surprise, "Uh, yes, a long time ago."

"Well, Roy and I were thinking it would be the best thing to help calm you down and perhaps you could take a nap as well."

"Oh, I don't know," Echo said. Normally, she would have gladly accepted, but she was afraid it would make her notice how upset she was even more.

"I've blended it with a few other herbs, which will help calm your nerves," Roy said.

Echo looked over at Dean. "Are you going to share this delightful herb with me?" she asked him, managing a smile.

"I can't," said Dean. "I'm in charge of the others. Gotta keep my head clear. But I'm sure Roy will." Dean looked over at Roy, who was already loading a small wooden pipe.

"You bet," said Roy. He winked at Echo. She got no impression he was being deceitful.

Echo sighed. "Okay, why not?"

"Good," said Dean. He stood up.

"Will you at least stay here for a bit?" Echo asked Dean.

He sat down again. "Sure, Strand, if that's what you want."

Echo practically choked on the first toke. Dean and Roy chuckled. "You want a water pipe?" Roy asked. "Sorry, I should have thought of that.

Echo waved her hand indicating no. When she caught her breath, she said, "Just not used to it. Gotta take in more air. Haven't had any of this stuff for about three years."

Roy took the pipe back, took a deep toke, held his breath, then handed it back to Echo.

Echo took another toke, and then stood up to use the facility. It was then the effects of the plant struck her. She was stoned. It was a familiar feeling, yet the circumstances were different. The fact that she was at a stranger's house, had lost her captain, and was possibly in an alternate universe, hit her all at once. She sat back down.

"You okay, Strand?" Dean asked.

"No, not really."

"What's going on?" Dean said.

"This whole situation is so bizarre."

"You want something to drink?" Roy asked. "A beer? Shot of tequila?"

Echo shook her head. "No, just water will be fine."

Roy got up and went to get the water. While he was gone, Echo took the opportunity to talk to Dean alone. How could she start the conversation though?

"Dean, I seem to have developed a heightened intuitive ability. Not because of the marijuana. You know when I said to unload the truck?"

Dean nodded.

"Well, I swear I didn't know it was going to blow up. I just sensed danger."

Dean was frowning, looking more thoughtful than doubtful, but Echo could see a trace of doubt in his face. "Okay," he finally said.

"And the captain, Dana, your sister, has acquired some energy healing ability. In the cave I had chills, and they went away when she touched me. Lucy had severe abdominal pain, and she was better after Dana covered her abdomen with her hands. This all started after the electrical storm when we were in the cave."

"Um-hmm. Anything else?"

"Yeah. Lucy could speak English after that too."

Was Dean trying to be open and receptive to what she said, because he didn't object to any of it? "Well, nothing different happened to me, or as far as I know, to Jamey or Amando."

"Maybe it only happens to females."

"Maybe."

"What I'm getting at is I think it's possible we were catapulted into an alternate timeline or universe or something like that." Echo put up her hand to prevent any objections he might have. "Just think about it—they use plastic cards to ID people as well as for credit. And Dana is accused of murder. How weird is that? And look at that flag on the wall—it only has fifty stars."

Before Dean could respond, Roy came through the door with a pitcher of water and three glasses.

"Where'd you get this marijuana?" Echo asked him. "It's good." She was starting to relax.

"I grow it out back in my greenhouse."

"Wow, aren't you afraid of getting busted?"

Roy laughed. "Of course not. It's legal."

"Oh right—Nevada," Echo said, remembering Nevada had legalized the plant many years ago.

"Not just Nevada. All fifty states have legalized it. Where've you been?"

Echo glanced at Dean and he caught her eye. Fifty states. "Been out in space too long," Echo said.

Roy poured them each a glass of water. It was clean and cold and refreshing.

"Are the others keeping busy?" Dean asked Roy.

"The kids are playing video games and Amando is walking around outside. I think he's getting restless."

Dean stood up. "Well, I'd better go out and keep him company."

Roy stood and closed the blinds on the windows. "You'd better get some sleep, Strand," he said.

"Yeah, I guess so." Echo wondered how she could sleep with all the questions floating around in her mind.

The men left the room and Echo went into the adjoining facility. She was shocked seeing her blonde hair. She'd forgotten she'd bleached it. She splashed water on her face. Her eyes were slightly bloodshot from the marijuana. Geez, I'm in bad shape, she thought. Gotta get some sleep.

The bed was comfortable even though it was a singlewide futon. She climbed into it, clothing and all, only having removed her shoes. It seemed like a long time before she sunk into sleep.

When Echo woke, she'd been dreaming of the captain. "I'm okay, Echo," she said instead of calling her "Strand." That's all Echo remembered. It took her several minutes to remember where she was. She sat up but was groggy.

Echo quickly washed up and left the bedroom. "Hello," she yelled. No one seemed to be around. She checked the common room, kitchen and other bedrooms. Then she went outside the front door. The van was gone. Her heart sank. She went around to the back of the house. "Hello," she yelled again several times. Finally, Roy emerged from his greenhouse.

"Strand," he said. "You're awake."

"Where are the others?" she said without bothering to acknowledge that yes, she was awake.

Roy stomped through the tall grass/weed combination that filled his yard, coming toward her. He removed his gloves, walked past Echo, and opened the back door, which led into a sort of mudroom. He stomped the dirt off his boots but did not remove them. Echo followed him into the kitchen. "Where are they?" she asked again, this time more urgently.

"Calm down, Strand," he said.

"Well?"

He sat at the wooden picnic-style table that ran the length of the windows. "They went to get Dana."

"What?" Why didn't anyone wake me? I wanted to help break her out."

"Sit down, my dear."

I'm not your dear, Echo thought, but she kept her mouth shut and sat in one of the plastiwood chairs.

Roy chuckled. "No breaking in or out was necessary. The FBI released her."

Instantly relieved, Echo felt the muscles in her face relax. "But how?"

"Seems her prints and DNA didn't match what they had on file for Dana Stewart. Plus, she was going by one of the alias IDs I made for her. But they are still looking for the "real" Dana Stewart.

Echo was wordless. How could that be unless—unless there were other versions of ourselves that belong in this universe?

"You look perplexed, my dear." This time Roy's "my dear" didn't bother her.

"I am." Echo thought a moment before speaking. "Did Dean happen to tell you my theory about us being from an alternate universe?"

Roy took a deep breath, and his expression turned serious. "He did."

"Well, what do you think?"

"I think it's entirely possible. I've heard of such things happening to people."

"So how do we get back?"

Roy leaned back and steepled his fingers together. "Now that's beyond my expertise. I do know that you must try to recreate the conditions that brought you over in the first place."

"And what happens if we don't go back?"

"I really don't know, but I've heard stories. These stories could be pure fiction. It's probably best I don't tell you."

Echo leaned over the table and gave him a good stare. "Tell me. I need to know."

Chapter 6
Together Again

After Roy told Echo he'd heard of a kind of physical degradation effect that happened to people who'd crossed universes, she really wished he hadn't told her. What did that mean? She wasn't sure she wanted to know. She felt anxiety grip her and her heart pounded. She went back into the bedroom and tried to comm her mother. Fortunately, she remembered her number. All her numbers were stored in her wristcomm she'd left back home. At once, after she dialed her mother's number, an automated voice responded that she'd dialed one too many numbers. "No such number exists. Try fewer numbers," the message said. She left the last number off on her next try and got an irritated old woman on the other end.

Dean had programmed all the group's numbers into the comms he had given them. Echo tried Dean. He answered immediately.

"What's up, Strand?" he asked abruptly.

Echo didn't want to come across as whiny, but she was quite upset he hadn't awakened her to go fetch the captain. On top of that, he'd left her alone with Roy, someone she didn't know very well.

"Where are you?" Echo asked. She couldn't quite hide the irritation in her voice.

"We'll be there in a little under an hour, Strand. I'll explain everything then." Dean clicked his comm off as abruptly as he'd answered it.

While Echo waited for the others to return, she used Roy's computer to look up her mother's number.

"Mom?"

"Echo, is that you?"

"Yes, Mom. I tried to comm you earlier, but I was given the message there was no such number."

"That's odd. I haven't changed my number. Where are you?"

"I'm near Reno, Nevada. We'll be heading out for Canada soon."

"I see." Her mother, Eudora, knew better than to pry into Echo's affairs, but Echo could tell by the tone of her voice and her hesitation to ask more details, that she was certainly open to Echo telling her more.

"How's Clark?" Echo wasn't sure if Clark was in the army in this timeline, but it turned out that he was.

"He's doing well. He's still stationed at Fort Benning, Georgia."

"Infantry?"

"No Echo—that's where infantry are trained, but Clark is still a cook." In her timeline, Clark was in the Army Corps of Engineers building housing for troops.

"Oh, right." Neither of them spoke for a moment.

"Have you contacted your father? I'm sure he'd like to hear from you."

Echo swallowed hard and dry, which left a lump in her throat. Her father had died in her timeline. "Uh, no. Do you have his number? I don't have my original comm."

"So that's why your ID didn't show up on my comm when you called."

"Yeah, I've got a cheap disposable one."

"Oh dear, I certainly hope no one got ahold of the information on it."

"No, it will only work with my voiceprint."

"Oh, right."

"Mom, Dad's number?"

"Oh, yes, yes. It's CH36204.

"Thanks, Mom. I'll contact you again when I can."

"Good-bye dear."

Echo's heart was pounding. She couldn't wait to call her father. She started to dial in the number, and then hesitated. She would eventually have to go back to her own timeline if she didn't want a premature death from physical degradation in this one. If she talked to or yet even saw her father, she wouldn't want to leave. What to do? This whole line of thinking made her extremely nervous.

While Echo was pondering her dilemma, she heard a vehicle roll up into Roy's graveled driveway. She ran to the window. It was the van. She dashed to the back door and opened it, watching Dean, Amando, Jamey, Lucy, and the captain pour out. She stuffed the comm into her pocket as they filed into the house.

Roy came up behind Echo. "Welcome back, friends."

Everyone looked tired, but the captain was more noticeably tired and stressed. Her face was gray and drawn. Echo had never seen her like this. Must be the timeline, she thought. Echo wanted to hug her; she was so relieved she was back. But the captain just said, "Hi, Strand," brushed past her, and flopped down onto the couch.

All of them gathered in the common room. Roy prepared some coffee and tea, and they began discussing their situation. To Echo's surprise, Jamey and Lucy seemed to accept their being in an alternate universe just fine. In fact, they thought it was cool.

"We'll have to find a way back," the captain said. "Pretty soon our health will deteriorate and we'll degrade faster than we should. I'm already feeling the effects."

"How do we get back?" Amando said.

Roy interjected. "I know a physicist in B.C., just outside Vancouver. He may be able to help."

"So, you mean we each have another version of ourselves in this reality?" Echo asked no one in particular.

"Possibly," Dean said.

"Probably," said the captain. "There's another version of me the FBI is looking for—the version that actually killed Jump Davis."

"My father is alive," Echo said. Everyone looked her way. "I spoke to my mother. Of course, her comm number was different, but she gave me my dad's number."

"Have you commed him yet?" Dean said.

"No, but I'd like to see him before we attempt to go back to our own time." Dean looked at the captain.

"Not a good idea, Strand," the captain said.

Echo's heart fell. She thought of the implications, the complications. If her father had seen the version of her recently and/or regularly, and then saw this version of her, he might not know what to think. He might ask her questions she didn't want to answer. He would expect her to know what he'd been up to. And she would probably look a little different than this reality's version did. She might even look older to him than her twenty-six years. But she wanted to see him so much that she'd be willing to take the risks.

"I could tell him the truth," Echo said.

The captain shrugged. "It's up to you, Strand. I'm not going to try and stop you, but I highly advise against it. We're all going to see the physicist. We can't wait for you to go see your father. You'd be separated from us."

"Unless I get my father to meet me in B.C."

"Well, that is an option," she said. "However, you could suffer long-term if not permanent emotional damage by separating from him. You'd go through the grief all over again that you experienced when he died."

"Maybe, but at least I'd see some version of him alive."

"It's up to you, Strand."

"What about you, Captain?"

"What about me?"

"Do you know where your daughter is in this reality?"

The captain took a deep breath and looked Echo straight in the eye. "I have no daughter in this reality."

Echo was about to ask her how she knew, but the captain gave her a steel-eyed stare as if to say, don't ask. Then her eyes softened.

"I used the public comms to try and find her. Then I checked the public birth records. She was not born here. The captain tried to look neutral, but Echo saw a glint of sadness in her eyes.

"We'll just have to find a way back to our time," said Echo. "There has to be a way." She tried to feel strong and confident, but she had doubts.

Chapter 7
On to Canada

Echo's stomach was still tied in knots as they crossed the border into Oregon. They had to get out of the van and wait while their identities were checked. This would be a good time to contact her father, but she couldn't decide whether to or not. Public comm stations were only several meters away. Using one of those, she could actually see him on video. Roy had set up a small line of credit for each of the adults in their group. Jamey and Lucy had been given some cash to play video games and get snacks. Amando, Dean, and the captain sat quietly, waiting. Echo flipped through a magazine reader, not really paying attention to what she was looking at. The captain glanced over at her from time to time, seeming to watch what she might do. Echo knew her nervousness showed. Finally, she could stand it no longer. She jumped up and headed for the public comms. The captain didn't try to stop her, but Echo knew she disapproved.

Echo's hand was shaking as she inserted the credit card into the machine. She tried several times and got an error message until she realized she'd put the card in the wrong way. She flipped it around and got a "connect" signal right away. She slowly dialed the prefix and number: CH36204. She held her breath. After several nerve-wracking seconds, she heard a click and then a voice: "Joe Strand," the voice said quickly, abruptly. Echo let out her breath. For a moment she considered hanging up.

Echo flipped on her screen. So what if he saw her blonde hair? "Dad?"

Joe Strand stared at his daughter for a moment, studying her. "Echo? Is that you?"

"Yes, Dad. How are you?" Seeing him alive and healthy stopped her breathing.

"Just fine, but you don't look so good. Are you all right?"

Echo let out her breath. "Ah, yes, of course. It's just so good to see you, Dad."

"So how's your trip going? Your mom said you were off on a road trip."

"Yes. I'm in Oregon on the way to Canada." This had been her plan in the other timeline, and evidently it was in this one as well.

"I hope you can still come to my barbeque when you get back to California."

Echo hesitated. "Uh, of course. When is the date again?"

"Echo, it's not like you to forget. We always have our barbeque on the last Saturday in October. Your mother and I will be expecting you."

"Yeah, I guess my mind has been occupied with this trip."

"I must go now. You take care of yourself, Echo."

"I will, Dad. See you soon." Echo reluctantly disconnected. She felt a hand on her shoulder, gentle, then gone. At first she was startled, but then relaxed. The captain was standing behind her.

"So, you saw your father."

Tears welled up in Echo's eyes, but she forced herself not to cry. She turned to face the captain. "Yes. I had to."

The captain put her arm around Echo's shoulders. "I understand, but you know we have to get back to our universe or we'll die."

"I just wish—."

"I know. C'mon, we've got to say our good-byes to Roy and leave for B.C."

The group drove north through Oregon and Washington State where their identities were checked again. A few hours later they reached the Canadian border at British Columbia. When they arrived, they were surprised that upon entering Canada, all vehicles were detained at large parking garages. Evidently, private vehicles were banned on public roads, at least in British Columbia. Well, if they were transported back to their own universe, they probably wouldn't be taking the van with them anyway.

Chapter 8
Fading Out/Fading In

Dana Stewart was not used to being scared. At least, she wasn't used to acknowledging her fear. She'd been in many situations where she didn't have time to be scared. She'd had to take charge of those situations in a hurry. Like the time she had to evacuate all the crew and passengers on the TransCom spaceplane she piloted to the moon. The ship had depressurized just as they reached the lunar station. And the time she and her crew were detained by NorCom Corporation at the moon when they announced they had taken over USSA, the United States Space Agency. But the situation she was in now—all six of them were in—was like no other she had experienced. Being stuck in some kind of alternate universe, losing physical integrity, and not knowing whether or not they could all get back to their own universe, had Captain Stewart very worried.

"All right, everyone," said the professor. "I've recreated the weather conditions as accurately as possible when the storm hit the night you were transported to this timeline."

Professor Aldous Huntsinger had been recommended to them by Roy, who seemed to have special contacts in the U.S. as well as Canada. The professor worked these "special cases" out of the basement of his home.

"I've done three other transports," he said, "but I can't tell you for sure if the people got back to their own timelines. However, as far as I can tell, they disappeared from this one, so the best I can do is wish you luck."

Not very comforting, but we have no choice, Dana thought. Her confidence once more surfaced and she was ready. "Let's do it then," she said.

Dean had used his credit card for the taxi that took them some fifty kilometers from the Canadian border to the professor's home. Then they'd had to wait over an hour for the professor to return home from the university. His wife, Amanda, was gracious to them, offering them tea and pastries, but the young people of the group, Jamey and Lucy, became restless. Amanda offered them a basketball they could play with outside in the driveway where a hoop was mounted over the garage door.

When the professor finally arrived home, the kids came in with him. He was not what Dana expected a professor to look like. He was young, perhaps in his mid-thirties. That would explain his young, handsome wife, though older men often had young wives. His skin was medium brown, like most of the population of North America. His hair was light, almost blond, and trimmed short. He wore no facial hair. However, in keeping with the old stereotype of a professor, his clothing was casual—slacks and a cardigan sweater with worn elbow patches over a dark green shirt.

Now he was ready to transport them. The kids didn't appear to be afraid, but they were certainly alert to what was happening.

"The booth has room for only three people. I'm going to leave it up to you folks who goes first."

Dana's thoughts raced. They'd left their van at the border. Dean had the key. What if the second transport put them into a completely different timeline? What if none of them reached their original timeline?

She felt a hand take hers. "It'll be okay, Captain," Strand said. Dana relaxed. That was a change—Strand comforting her instead of the other way around.

Dana looked to her brother for a decision. After a few seconds he said, "Ladies first." That meant Lucy, Strand, and Dana would step into the cylindrical container first. Might as well get it over with, she thought. This experiment cost them their last four bars of uzerium. Anyway, they couldn't take it with them. The professor said it was too dense for transport. They could take only the clothing on their backs and their shoes. That meant they would arrive back in their own timeline with only their fake credit cards for money. Or maybe they'd just be transported back in time. If so, their wristcodes would work again. Dana still had a few hundred credits in her account. The U.S. president had quickly realized the country couldn't function on currency alone, as she had wanted. So, when Dana and her crew got back from their one-year mission to the asteroid belt, she'd immediately re-established her bank account and reactivated her wristcode. Dean had not. He had erased his wristcode years ago, protesting the government and the corporations. In their original timeline, Dean had insisted on using currency or uzerium, as he didn't trust the banks or the government that was supposed to insure the banks.

Dana stepped into the transparent cylinder first, followed by Strand and Lucy. Lucy, holding Strand's hand, looked longingly at Jamey. If things went wrong, she might never see him again. Dana took Lucy's hand as well as Strand's, so they were all connected. The three of them kept their eyes on the three guys outside the container. As the cylinder doors started to slide closed, Lucy screamed. The professor opened the doors again. Lucy let go of Dana and Strand and rushed out of the cylinder toward Jamey. Dana and Strand stepped out as well. Jamey had a shocked look on his face. His right hand and part of his arm had faded out, as if it were a hologram. Lucy touched it, and her hand went right through his. The physical degradation had begun.

"We need to put the boy in the cylinder first," the professor said. One of you must trade places with him."

"I will," Dana said. "Hurry, get into the cylinder." Jamey and Lucy rushed into the container, but Strand hesitated. "That means you too, Strand." We'll catch up with you." Dana gently pushed a reluctant Strand into the container. The doors slid closed. The professor punched a button, and the cylinder became enclosed in a white fog. Dana held her breath while the fog slowly dissipated. The cylinder was empty.

"Okay, your turn. You'd better hurry." Dean's left arm was fading like Jamey's right hand did. He rushed the remainder of the group into the cylinder. They didn't have time to take one another's hands before the doors closed and the fog encircled them.

At first Dana felt as if she were waking from an unconscious state. She was standing, but a white fog was surrounding her. She reached out in all directions with both arms, but she could not feel Amando or Dean. Her feet felt like they were on a rocky surface, unlike the padded surface in the cylinder. And she was cold to the point of shivering.

Slowly, the fog dissipated. She ventured to take a few steps, but the ground was sharp and uneven, and she nearly fell. As she steadied herself, a hand grabbed her arm. She was startled at first and tried to pull her arm free. But the hand held her tightly.

"Dana, it's okay." Through the remaining fog she recognized the face of her brother. Thank goodness, she was not alone.

"Where are the others?" Dana asked.

"I don't know, but I think we're back in the cave."

Dana's mind raced. Had they also gone back in time? She looked at her clothing. She was no longer dressed like a man, and her western boots were gone, replaced by her black hiking boots. And she was wearing her USSA flight jacket. She felt her hair. It was shoulder length again. They must have gone back in time. What if the others didn't show up? Would they be cast into yet another timeline?

"Señor Dean," a voice called out.

"Amando! Over here," Dean called. Now the fog was almost gone. Dana saw that she and Dean were standing next to the fire pit where they'd eaten the wonderful vegetable stew. Amando was standing on the ridge where Dana and Strand had slept the night of the storm.

Amando joined Dana and Dean. "Vaya mirar fuera," Dean told Amando. Amando went to the cave opening and looked around outside, shrugged, and turned back.

Then Dana pointed to the back of the cave. "The truck is there!" Astonished, Dean and Dana rushed to the truck and searched inside. There, in the back under several layers of blankets, they found Strand, Lucy, and Jamey.

"They're asleep," said Dana.

"Or dead," Dean said.

After checking their pulses and finding them alive, Dean and Dana woke the three of them. It wasn't an easy task. Gently, Dana took rocked Strand's shoulders until her eyes opened. "We're safe. It's okay." Strand moved her head back and forth slowly, and then attempted to sit up. Dana had to help her. Once Strand was awake, Dana woke Lucy, while Dean woke Jamey. They all were wearing the clothing they had on when they first stayed in the cave. Strand's hair was light brown again.

"Where are we?" Jamey said.

"Back in the cave. You're in the truck."

"The one that blew up?"

"Yes. We probably went back in time."

The rest of the group stumbled out of the truck, still groggy from the temporal transport. Strand looked around the cave, and then examined each of the others. "The carvings on the wall are the same as they were before the electrical storm," she said.

Then Dean jumped up and slid under the truck. He proceeded to check every area of the truck, inside and out. "They had to have planted it somewhere we can't detect," he said. "We have no scanners, no comms, no electronic devices to detect a bomb. They could have hidden the bomb inside the axle or the tranny or anywhere it could not be seen. If we did go back in time, and I believe we did, we have about sixteen hours before this thing explodes. We're going to have to get rid of this truck, soon."

"Let's drive to Reno now," said Dana. We can use the Faraday shields to prevent any EMF from the storm kicking us into another timeline."

"Or maybe it had to do with the cave," Strand said.

"What?" said Dana.

"Us going into that alternate timeline. What if the storm created a vortex inside the cave?"

"Maybe, but we shouldn't take any chances," said Dean. "The shields will use up a lot of power, but we can make it to Reno with the hydro backup. Then I'll drive it out into the desert away from the city and hitch a ride back. Of course, we'll unload the uzerium first."

Dana was impatient. "Dean, I'm grateful for all your help." She looked around at the others. "You all have been very supportive, but I'm tired of being on the run. I'm going to rent a plane, fly myself to Vancouver, and see that doctor. The rest of you can go home. I don't want to jeopardize your lives in case Davis or his people find me—and they probably will."

"I'm going with you," Dean said immediately. "I'm only a few hundred kilometers northeast of Vancouver.

Dana hesitated. "I wish you'd take a commercial flight."

Before Dean could reply, Strand stepped forward. "I'm going with you, Captain, and don't try to stop me."

Dana lightly touched her arm and looked her in the eye. "No. I need you to go back to California with Lucy, Amando, and Jamey. Then she turned to Amando and Jamey. Would you two be willing to accompany Lucy back to Mexico to reunite her with her family?"

"Sí," said Amando. Jamey looked over at Lucy and nodded.

Strand started to object, but Dana stopped her. "Plus, I need you to tell Wilson what's been going on. I still don't want to risk comming him."

"All right. If that's what you want."

"It's what I want and *need* from you, Strand."

Just then, a bolt of thunder hit, followed by a flash of lightning at the cave's entrance.

"We've got to get out of here now!" Dean said. "Everyone in the truck."

They all piled into the truck—Amando in the driver's seat, Dean and Dana in the front, while the rest of them jumped into the back with all the supplies. Amando nicked the front right fender as they exited the cave, but that didn't stop or slow them down. It was dark outside except for the occasional lightning flashes that struck in sheets. Dana wished she had climbed into the back so she couldn't see the danger they were in with the rain now coming down on the narrow dirt road as they wound over the mountain and headed for the interstate.

Chapter 9
Dallas and Slug

Dallas Jones sat at the bar in the casino drinking soda water and watching her partner, Herbert "Slug" Spillman gamble away his cash at the roulette table. They had each been given a three thousand dollar cash advance from Jump Davis to kidnap Dana Stewart. Dallas didn't like the idea of being involved in abducting a USSA captain, but she needed the money because she had quit her own USSA job. She hadn't said anything about that to Slug, who had been involved in criminal activities before—once a bank robbery when he'd killed a teller, and another time when he'd shot a cop. Dallas was in danger by just being with him.

Dallas tried to focus on the half-million cash reward she and Slug were to split once they turned Stewart over to Davis. But who knew when the group would show up in Reno, if at all? They carried no comms, no GPS, no electronics that could point anyone to their position.

"Damn," Slug said as he stomped over to the bar and sat down next to Dallas. He looked at her pleadingly.

"Oh no you don't. It was your decision to gamble, and you're not taking one dollar of mine."

"But Dal, I can win it back. I'll play a lower risk game like Black Jack. Please!"

Dallas sighed. "I guess I'll never hear the end of it if I don't give you something."

Slug's face lit up, as Dallas dug into her pocket and pulled out several bills. She handed a twenty-five dollar bill to Slug. He pretended to pout.

"That's it, and no more drinks. I mean it, Slug. We've got to be alert when Stewart shows up. In fact, we should get out of here now and scope the streets for that truck."

"Just a few games of Black Jack to win back your money. Be right back."

Dallas sighed. "Just don't be too long, or I'm leavin' without you." She pulled their vehicle's key card out of her jacket pocket and dangled it in front of him.

"No problem."

Dallas turned toward the bartender. "Another club soda please."

As she sat and watched the gamblers, she thought about her days of recklessly drinking and trying almost any recreational drug that came her way. What a waste. Now, she prided herself on being drug-free and sober. She had an occasional beer, but didn't make a habit of it. She had tried gambling a few times, but it never appealed to her. As she sat and waited for Slug, her anger grew. She would have to take charge of this operation now, and they would have to wait until Slug sobered up.

Just then, Slug returned with an exuberant smile on his face and was waving his arms. "I won, Dallas!" He flashed a fist full of cash in front of her face. She was not impressed.

"Okay, let's get out of here." Dallas stood up. Slug looked longingly at the roulette table, but Dallas grabbed his arm and turned him the other way. "Forget it."

Back at the hotel, Slug opened the safe and removed the two pistols. "Okay, let's go get that captain," he said as he stumbled to the bed and sat down, admiring the guns.

Dallas grabbed them from his hands. "Not in your condition."

"Come on, I'm in the mood." Slug made a gun gesture with his hand, pointing his finger toward the large mirror on the wall.

"You're going to sober up first. Maybe tomorrow." She put the guns back into the safe and closed the door.

Slug protested and danced around the room for a while, releasing his excess energy. Dallas turned on the wallscreen and finally got Slug to settle down, first sitting him on the bed, then forcing him to lie down and pulling off his shoes. She hoped he didn't get sick, but he rarely did. He could hold his liquor pretty well. Plus, she'd made him drink some Sober-Quik. However, it was already past 9:00 p.m., and it would be best to start in the morning.

Dallas sat on her bed watching the wallscreen, but really not focusing on its information. She channel-surfed for a while, but was really thinking about her past. She had been so loyal to USSA. She'd gone on every mission they'd assigned to her team. Had never taken a sick day, even when she hadn't felt that well. She had risen in rank from ensign to lieutenant commander in less than two years. She was acting first officer for several months after that. When the captain vacancy came up, she was sure she'd be promoted, but a man from another team was assigned—Coop Wilson, Captain Stewart's first officer. She was enraged. Not only that, she was jealous of all the attention Stewart and her ensign, Echo Strand, had gotten for repairing the solar power satellite and restoring power to the western U.S. grid.

Dallas lay in bed trying to figure out just what to do if and when she found Stewart. She and Slug would have to get her alone. That wouldn't be easy. The only thing Dallas could think of was if Stewart went into a public facility by herself. Dallas would make sure both their pistols were locked on stun. She wasn't going to be a murderer or party to a murder. Once unconscious, they could drag Stewart out a back door and transfer her to their vehicle in the alley. That was if everything went as planned and the conditions were right. But hell, she didn't even know if Stewart was in Reno or would even be stopping here. Her mind finally gave up trying to figure things out, and she drifted off to sleep.

The next morning, Dallas flipped on the wallscreen and turned to the local broadcast news station while Slug was in the shower washing away his hangover. She sat up straighter as the news showed that an abandoned deuce-and-a-half blew up in the desert just outside of Reno. She had no idea Slug had placed an explosive in the truck when he installed the tracking device. She was extremely relieved that no one was in the truck when it blew.

We've got to get going, she thought. They're probably headed for Reno—or they're already here. The destroyed vehicle was reported found early that morning at 4:37 a.m. Maybe they've gone to the airport or acquired another vehicle, she thought. Reno was a small town compared to some, but not *that* small. She momentarily set aside her anger with Slug. Her mind raced. She and Slug could split up—comb the hotels, restaurants, and casinos.

Dallas pounded on the facility room's door. "C'mon, Slug. Hurry up. We've got to get moving."

Around noon, after searching the streets all morning, Slug and Dallas met up at a small café to grab a bite and discuss their situation. They sat in a booth near the back of the restaurant. Dallas was chowing down on her burger—she was famished—when Slug's eyes popped open.

"Don't turn around, whatever you do."

Dallas dropped her burger onto her plate. "What?" she asked in a voice muffled by the food still in her mouth. She hurried to chew it up.

"The booth kitty-corner to us. There's a woman who looks like Stewart. But there's a kid sittin' next to her—looks Mexican, eleven or twelve years old."

Dallas swallowed and wiped her face with a napkin. "You stay right here." She picked up her cup. "I'm going to go get some more coffee."

"Okay, but don't do anything stupid."

Dallas frowned at Slug. "You are not calling *me* stupid. I'm not the one who gambled away his earnings."

"Hey, I got your money back."

Dallas stood up. "We'll discuss this later." She sauntered over to the counter and stole a glance at the people in the booth. It sure did look like Stewart. But there were six people crowded into the booth. She took her time adding cream and sugar, which she normally didn't use, to her coffee, and then she casually wandered back to her table. She could see another person in the booth, and that person resembled Echo Strand. She'd never met Strand or Stewart in person, but they sure looked like the vid clips Davis had given them.

"Well?" Slug asked when she returned.

"I think it's them, but there are six of them including two kids." But why would they abandon the truck out in the desert unless they suspected a bomb?"

"Listen, we'll wait until they get up to leave. I've got a plan."

"What?" Slug scraped the remains of the pancake syrup off his plate and licked it off his fork.

"Just stay put."

As the group began to vacate their booth, Dallas, timing her move very carefully, rushed toward them and forcefully bumped into Stewart, slipping a small tracker into her jacket pocket. "Sorry, Ma'am," she said. She got a good look at the face. It *was* Captain Stewart.

Chapter 10
Flight Check

Dana sat at the controls of the two-person private single-engine jet plane. She was going through the preflight check with Dean when her palms began to burn. She shook her hands and inspected her palms. They looked normal, but the burning sensation increased.

"Get me water now!" she told Dean.

"What's wrong?"

"I don't know." She blew on her palms, first her right, then her left, back and forth until Dean produced a drinking bottle. She grabbed it from him and squirted each palm. The burning ceased immediately. She handed the bottle back to Dean and wiped her hands on her jeans.

"What is it?" Dean asked.

"My hands—they were burning up."

"You okay now?" he said, concerned.

"Yeah. I don't know what that was."

Dana hadn't flown one of these mini-jets for several years, but she'd kept up her rating by periodically practicing in a simulator. Dean had flown one similar to this one a few times but didn't have enough hours to go solo. He was a good backup in case something happened to Dana during the flight.

While they were waiting in line for takeoff from the Reno Regional Airport, Dana wondered if her healing abilities were still working now that she was back in her own timeline. At least she was pretty certain they were all back in their own timeline. Their currency worked—that was a good sign. Also, her wristcode was active, and she had credit in the bank. Perhaps the healing abilities still did work. Maybe the heat in her hands had something to do with that. Her thoughts were interrupted by the announcement in her earplug that she was cleared for takeoff.

Down the runway they went. The thrill of taking off still filled her with excitement, even though she'd done it hundreds of times. Once in the air, there wasn't much to do. She hadn't been to Canada for almost two years. It would be cold there, and she wasn't used to that. Dean promised he'd go with her to the professor, who was also a doctor, to have the implant removed, but then he needed to get home to his wife, who had been taking care of their herbal botanical medicinal plants all on her own. Dana would still have a partial artificial brain, but the implant that powered her brain would be taken out, and they had been told the professor would be able to make her brain run independently.

About a half hour into the flight, Dana sneezed. She hadn't done that in a very long time, since the implant and her bionic brain parts had kept her well and healthy. But maybe that had changed since the shift to the alternate timeline and back.

"You okay?" Dean asked.

Dana shrugged. "It's a little chilly up here. Must've made me sneeze."

Dean turned up the heat. Dana fished in her pocket for a handkerchief. She usually carried one, as it came in handy for numerous things like wiping condensation off windows or cleaning up spilled coffee. As she was shaking out the folded hanky, something fell onto the floor. Dean bent over and picked it up. He held it out in his open hand. It was a small red dot blinking on and off.

"A transmitter or tracking device," Dean said, clearly alarmed. "Someone must have slipped it into your pocket."

Dana took it from him and examined it as if it could tell her where it had come from. She thought for a moment, and then spoke. "That woman in the café. She bumped into me."

"And dropped the tracker into your pocket."

"We've got to get rid of it."

"Yeah, but we can't open the window at ten thousand meters."

"I know." Dana dropped the tracker to the floor of the airplane and stomped on it with the heel of her boot. The small device didn't break, but the light stopped blinking.

Dean laughed. "Well, that's one way to do it."

"Hand me that water bottle." Dean passed the small water container to his sister. She plopped the tracker into it and shook the bottle. "Just in case," she said.

After they arrived at the Vancouver Airport and went through Customs, Dean rented a car for the drive to the university.

"Well, this is another clue we're in the right timeline again," said Dean. Private vehicles are allowed on the city streets."

"Yeah, and the traffic congestion that goes with it," Dana said.

"Are you nervous about the procedure?"

"A little, I guess, but I also am looking forward to getting rid of this implant. Thanks for paying for the rental car."

"No problem."

"And for helping me out with the truck and all that."

"My pleasure. Anything for my older sister," Dean said.

Dana smiled. "Yeah, older by five minutes."

"You used to rub that in all the time when we were kids."

"What can I say? We were kids."

Dean drove on to the electrically banded freeway. "Ah, how nice this ride is compared to that truck."

"You bet." Dana relaxed and let out a sigh.

Dean glanced over at Dana. Once on the freeway, he didn't have to keep his eyes on the road, since he'd programmed in his destination exit. "We could go to my house and do this tomorrow if you want."

"I know you're eager to get home, Dean. If you don't mind though, I just want to go see the professor and get this over with."

"That's fine, Dana." In a few minutes, the vehicle exited the freeway.

Chapter 11
Echo Goes Home

Echo, Jamey, Amando, and Lucy boarded the air train from Reno's train station. Dean had given Amando enough cash to take the three of them to Mexico and deliver Lucy back to her parents. Then Amando and Jamey would return to Canada. Evidently, he lived with Amando, his uncle on his mother's side because his mother had died and his father was an alcoholic who was unfit to care for Jamey. Echo didn't know the whole story, but she'd caught pieces of conversation from overhearing Dean tell the captain.

As they sat on the train, each of them seemed lost in their own worlds. So much had happened, and Echo just felt like quietly processing it all. She figured the others felt the same way. Lucy could still speak English, and Echo felt she'd gained a sort of calmness she hadn't had before. Whether Echo would still have the instant insight or intuitive ability she'd had in the other timeline just before the truck blew up, remained to be seen. But her calm mind made her feel as though she was more open to receiving those types of insights. For one thing, she knew she needed to have a long talk with Sanders, her domestic partner. They had become romantically involved during the long flight to the asteroid belt, and then moved in together when they got back.

Sanders had wanted to get married, but Echo was not in love with her. She wished she were, but she couldn't make that happen. Sanders was a good friend and companion, but the passion wasn't there. Echo's mind had been on the captain more than anyone—not in a romantic way, but with a strong sense of loyalty. The captain had also been a mentor to Echo. Echo foresaw them being friends—more equal now—even though Echo still felt very protective of her captain.

Echo didn't know what she wanted to do next. She was tired of being stuck in a spaceship for days on end, but she did like going out into space if she could return right away. And now she wanted to move away from Sanders. She kind of enjoyed this feeling though. Although it carried with it uncertainty, there was a kind of excitement about not knowing what she would do next. But she also wanted to stay close to the captain. It was a dilemma, because the captain was assigned long trips like going to Mars.

"Los Angeles stop in five minutes," the automated voice announced. "Be prepared to disembark." The announcement was then repeated in Spanish: "La parada del tren en los Angeles serà en cinco minutos. Preparece para desembarcar." Echo snapped awake from her musings. This would probably be the last time she'd see Amando, Jamey, and Lucy, unless some remote chance encounter brought them together again.

Everyone filed off the train and into the depot. Echo took Lucy's hand as Lucy took Jamey's. She wanted to stay with them as long as she could, which would only be thirty minutes before their train left for San Diego and then the Mexican border.

After the chaos of winding through the crowds and getting their luggage, they luckily found four seats together in the depot. At first, no one said anything. Then Echo spoke up. "I'm going to miss you all."

Silence, then, "Me too," said Lucy. She had let go of Echo's hand, but was still holding Jamey's. He seemed nervous. He let go of Lucy's hand, and then stood up abruptly. "Does anyone want something to drink?"

"Yeah, I'll take some water," Echo said.

"Sí por favor," said Amando. "Me too."

"No thanks," said Lucy.

Once Jamey was gone, Echo took Lucy's hand again. "You take care of yourself, kid."

Lucy looked at the floor then back at Echo. "I'll be okay." Tears started to well up in her eyes, but she held them back.

"Well, I'm sure you'll be glad to see your parents." Echo wanted to give the girl a hug, but she didn't want to embarrass her or make her cry.

"Jamey returned with two cups of water. He handed one to Echo and the other to Amando.

"Thanks, Jamey." Echo drank the entire cup of water. She was thirstier than she'd known.

Jamey sat down again between Amando and Lucy. "You don't have to wait around for us to leave," Jamey told Echo.

"I know," Echo replied. She briefly wondered if he wanted her to leave, but quickly dismissed the thought. Even if he did, she was going to stay with the group until they boarded their train. They'd been through a lot together, and though she was eager to go home and get her wristcomm, wash her clothes, and contact Wilson, she was reluctant to leave the people she'd shared jumping into an alternate universe with. Especially Lucy. Echo remembered being Lucy's age and how difficult it was dealing with her emotions. Echo had been very secretive—even more so than now. Now she still didn't want to show her feelings for fear of criticism. But she'd learned to toughen up, especially being the lowest ranking officer on Captain Stewart's space crew. She'd also witnessed the captain's daughter, Cheyenne, and her rebelliousness and moodiness, and had developed a modicum of compassion for teen behavior.

There was nothing to say. Echo didn't want to force any more conversation. So they sat and waited for the San Diego train. About ten minutes later, the announcement was made, and they all stood up abruptly. Before Amando, Jamey, and Lucy could grab their bags, Echo hugged Amando, then Jamey, then Lucy. She couldn't help herself. The gestures weren't planned—they were spontaneous.

"Bye, take care of yourselves," she told them as they walked away. They each acknowledged her with a wave of the hand. Lucy looked back at Echo as she walked away holding Jamey's hand. *I hope he stays* in touch with her, Echo thought. She stood there watching them until they disappeared from her sight.

Echo took a deep breath. She felt a little lightheaded and again wondered if she was really back in the right universe. She had so many people to contact—Coop Wilson, Jeremy, her longtime friend, and of course her mother—Eudora Wild and her brother, Clark Strand. She dreaded facing Sanders, but perhaps she could go to the apartment while Sanders was at work.

Echo caught a train to within two blocks of her apartment. Dragging her duffel bag a couple blocks wasn't too bad. The temperature was relatively cool at 70°F/21°C for Southern California. Echo climbed the stairs to the second level and found her door. She waved her wristcode over the brass plate on the door, and it swished open. She must be in the right universe for that to work. She breathed a sigh of relief that Sanders was not home. The sparsely furnished common room looked the same, with a single couch next to the north wall and two padded rocking chairs opposite the couch. The small wooden dining room table and chairs were neatly arranged with a tablecloth and fresh cut red carnations in a small glass vase. Wow, was Sanders acquiring a feminine touch?

Echo dumped out her duffel bag and started to do her laundry. Then she dug under her mattress to find her wristcomm. She turned it on, but though she'd had it charging all this time, the battery was low. She'd need to purchase a new one. That was a disappointment.

Several hours went by quickly. Echo had washed and folded her laundry and taken a much-needed shower. Oh crap, it was almost 4:00 p.m. Sanders would be home soon. Echo knew she was still in avoidance mode, but she didn't care. She'd come back later and talk to Sanders, not necessarily about breaking up with her, just about her trip. Right now, she needed to find Wilson and get a new battery for her wristcomm. Also, go to the bank and get some cash.

Echo found Wilson at the house he shared with the captain. He was up on a ladder painting the window trim.

"Wilson," Echo yelled. He didn't hear her, so she moved closer so that she was at the base of the ladder. She looked around at the yard. Flowers had been planted since she'd last been there. The lawn was freshly mowed. Wilson must still be on furlough. She yelled his name again. This time, he looked down. Once he recognized her, he quickly descended the ladder.

"Echo Strand!" He gave her a big hug.

"How are you, Wilson?" His eyes sparkled. He didn't look any different than the last time she'd seen him. His hair was a little shorter, but that was about it.

"Let me soak my paintbrush and wash my hands. C'mon in the house. I want to hear about everything. Where's Dana?"

"She's in Canada with Dean. They flew out on a private jet from Reno," she told him as they walked into the house and sat down at the kitchen table. It was a huge house with five bedrooms and three facilities. Echo had only been in it a couple times before. She wondered what they were going to do with all that room. She glanced into the common room and noticed the windows had been replaced since Davis' people had broken in.

"Want some coffee?" Wilson asked as he poured himself a cup.

"No thanks. Water'll be fine. I've been so thirsty lately."

"One water coming up," Wilson said cheerfully.

They sat at the kitchen table, and Echo told him the story, leaving out the part about the alternate universe. She'd let the captain fill him in on that.

"So, she's in Canada now," Wilson said. "Yeah, she said she'd come straight home when she was done with the procedure."

"Will she have to stay any length of time for recovery?"

Echo shrugged. "I don't know, but the way she was talking, it sounded like she was anxious to get home."

Wilson stood up but had a concerned look on his face. "Guess I'd better get back to work."

Echo stood as well. "Yeah, I gotta get a battery for my comm and get over to the base, check my schedule, and find some quarters for myself."

"You moving out from Sanders?"

Echo looked down at the floor and back at Wilson. "Yeah."

Wilson didn't inquire further.

"I'll tell you about it some time."

They both walked toward the front door. "Say, you can check your schedule from here if you'd like."

"Thanks, Wilson. I'll just do it there."

"Sure," he said as he opened the door. "Come back anytime."

"Will do."

"Oh, and Strand, I'll be putting up an invisible force field around the house in a day or two. It won't shock anyone, just bounce them gently away."

"Oh, I know the kind you mean. Thanks for letting me know."

"Yeah, just comm the house number."

"Okay. I'll be checking back soon to see if the captain is back."

"Okay." Wilson went outside with her. The air was clear and warm with a soft breeze, but Echo could still see that L.A. smog in the distance.

Once on the USSA base (yes her wristcode still worked there—she must be in the correct timeline) she took the maglev train to the base's gigantic warehouse and bought a battery for her wristcomm. She tested it before leaving and found it worked just fine. She didn't want to activate a holo-display on the train in front of other people, so she just waited until she got to Scheduling. She saw several people she knew, and they gave each other a passing "hi."

Her team was still on indefinite furlough. Because Wilson had moved on to a new team, Echo's team was going to be assigned a new first officer. Most everyone on furlough would have to find temporary jobs unless they had enough money to live on. And although the U.S. president initially banned using credit, she had limited it to new small businesses during the year Echo was away in the asteroid belt. Wristcodes were still debit only.

Echo found a private booth to activate the holo-images from her wristcomm. She had missed it while on the trip with the captain, Dean, and the others. Now that she had it back again, it felt like a lost companion that she never wanted to part with again.

When she accessed her bank account, Echo's heart jumped. The balance was almost ten times greater than she expected. Her first thought was that she was in the wrong universe. Perhaps most of it looked the same as when she left, but maybe there were only tiny details that were different. She had planned on getting a part-time job. Maybe even working in her mother's new grocery store out in the surrounds. There must be some mistake.

After putting in a second passcode, she was able to see a list of deposits and withdrawals. No activity for a couple of weeks except for the day before. A huge deposit of twenty thousand dollars had been made, but the depositor's name remained anonymous. Only a note had been made next to the deposit. It read, "thank you." Ah ha! It must've been Dean or the captain. Dean still had a lot of uzerium, and the captain had been paid handsomely (Echo didn't know how much but she knew it was a lot) for commanding the yearlong mission to the asteroid belt. That was why she could buy a house.

Well, Echo didn't have to get a job for a while. Twenty thousand dollars in this new economy where cola was ten cents a can, would go a long way. Now she would have time to move out of her apartment.

All of a sudden an alarming sensation overcame Echo. Something had happened to her mother. She didn't know what, but she felt an urgent need to get in touch with her. She'd look for an apartment later.

Echo commed her mother's number, but there was no answer. She had no idea where Clark was, but she tried her brother anyway. The number was no longer in service. Clark was in the Army Corps of Engineers the last time she'd seen him. She decided to try comming her mother's grocery store. She waited and waited until finally someone answered. It was a familiar voice of a young man.

"Jeremy?"

"Yes, is that you, Echo?"

"Jeremy, are you working there now?"

"Yes, I have been since right after you left on your trip."

"Well, that's great. Say, I'm looking for my mother. Is she there?"

There was a momentary pause from Jeremy's end. "Echo, she's in the hospital."

Echo gasped. "Since when? Where? What's wrong with her?"

"It's her heart, Echo. She needs a new one. She went in to Mercy General a few hours ago. They're growing her a new one, but it's going to take another week or so. You should go see her. She's been worried about you."

"Thanks, Jeremy. Thanks so much. I'm on my way."

Chapter 12
Dana's Discovery

Still not risking using their comms for fear of being tracked by Jump Davis or his people, Dana and Dean took a taxicab directly to the University of British Columbia Medical School where Dr. Roman Sanchez was supposedly employed. His name had been given to Dean as a specialist in "experimental" neurosurgery. That sounded a bit risky to Dana, but she didn't care. She wanted the implant out of her head. Her goal was to live out a normal lifespan, not hundreds of years as the continual replacement of her type of implant was supposed to provide. It kept the artificial parts of her brain functioning, which had given her optimal health and increased strength. If she had to give that up, so be it. Jump Davis wanted that implant. She also knew he was obsessed with her and angry enough with her for partnering up with Coop Wilson that he might kill her. Definitely a psychopath. The implant might even have a tracking device in it, but hopefully not. Without their communication devices, Dana and the others had successfully evaded Jump Davis. It was odd though, that since the group's timeline shift to the alternate universe and then back again, Dana had been able to sleep more hours than she'd been able to before. She'd also felt weaker physically, so something must have altered her body chemistry.

It had been years since Dana had been on the UBC campus. It had grown immensely. Most of the older buildings had been replaced with modern structures. She and Dean went to the main campus directory and searched for the Medical Research & Development Building. A holo popped out with precise directions. Since they had no mobile devices that could download this map, they requested a printout, which was expensive because it required ink and paper.

"Whew, ten dollars for this," Dean said.

"No problem, we can afford it," said Dana.

They both studied the map for a moment and then were on their way.

The medical school consisted of a series of smaller buildings connected together by tunnels, as it rained a lot in this part of the world. It took the twins a while to navigate the tunnels, sometimes getting lost, but they finally found Dr. Sanchez's office, one of a number of identical doors in a long hallway. Dean knocked on the door, but there was no answer. Then Dana pushed on the door to see if it was unlocked. It wasn't.

The two of them then found an office down the hall and inquired as to the whereabouts of Dr. Sanchez.

"Oh, he's teaching a class right now. His office hours today are," the receptionist quickly checked his computer, "from four to five p.m."

It was almost 1:00 p.m. now. "Let's go find a bite to eat," Dana suggested. In the Student Commons, they sat at a small booth, ambient noise around them, and somehow started talking of their childhood.

"I wonder why Mom and Dad moved to the states when we were only three years old, then moved back to Canada a year and a half later," Dana said.

"You know, Dad got that job in Seattle."

"Yeah, but why drag us along? Seattle was close enough for him to come home on the weekends."

Dean shrugged. "Guess he wanted his family with him. At least we all got duel citizenship out of it."

"Yeah, that's convenient." Dana finished the last of her tuna sandwich. "Wow, I was hungry."

"I really miss them," said Dean.

"Mom and Dad?"

He nodded. "More than ever."

"Me too."

"Every time I think about how they were murdered with that poisoned water, it makes me crazy angry." He hit his fist on the table but not too hard to draw attention.

"No use dwelling on it, Dean. What's done is done."

Dean sighed. "I know. At least it motivated me to become a leader in the Resistance."

"It did indeed. Too bad those corporate leaders had to murder our parents. And we still don't know who did it."

"Probably never will. The war between the corporations and the Resistance has seemed to have died down, but those corporations, though they've been broken up, have this tendency to merge quickly and this whole battle could start all over again."

"I hope not. I'm weary of all this fighting. I just want to go home, work on my house, and be with Wilson. I'd like to see Cheyenne too."

"I'm glad you recovered most of your memories since that horrid spaceplane accident. Dana, we've still got to do something about Jump Davis. He's not going to give up looking for you."

Dana waved her hand away. "That man is totally obsessed. What *can* we do?"

"Once you get that implant out of your head, we could somehow send it to him. That's what he's after."

"Yeah, if the professor lets us keep it."

"He'd better."

"Jump has a grudge against me, and he might still want to kidnap me, but I am so tired of running. Once the implant is removed, I'm going home. And you should too. Jane is probably out of her mind with worry."

"I hate to leave you on your own."

"I'll be okay. I'll just fly the mini-jet to Southern California and land at the base. High security there, you know."

"Then what?"

Dana shrugged. She scooped the crumbs from the table onto her plate, adding her coffee cup and napkin.

"Dana?"

"I'll figure that out when the time comes. You know, Dean, I *can* take care of myself."

"Yeah, I know. I just worry."

They both stood up. "You're the best brother anyone could ever have." She kissed his cheek.

"Oh stop it," Dean said playfully.

Dana laughed. "Should we head over to Sanchez's office?"

"It's only three-thirty."

"By the time we navigate those tunnels, it'll be four."

They waited by Dr. Sanchez's office door until he arrived at 4:10.

"How can I help you?" Sanchez asked after they were all seated in his office. He was younger than Dana had imagined, dark hair, slim, with a long, narrow face and medium brown skin.

Dana scanned the room. To her left she noticed what appeared to be some unfamiliar medical equipment. Sanchez even had a bookcase filled with actual physical paper books and journals.

Dean cleared his throat. "Sorry to come unannounced, but we were told that you might be able to remove an implant in my sister's head."

Sanchez studied Dana. "You look familiar."

Dana looked him directly in the eye, not at all timid. "I'm a captain with USSA. You may have seen me on broadcast news over a year ago."

Sanchez looked thoughtful. "Oh yes. You were portrayed as a hero of sorts for helping repair the solar power satellite."

"Yes." Dana didn't elaborate on her involvement with that. "My doctor, James Sereno, was unable to remove my implant, but he told me to contact you. He said you had researched a new technique to safely remove brain implants."

"Yes, I have performed six successful implant removals." Sanchez sat straight up in his chair eyeing both Dana and Dean.

After a moment, Dean asked, "Any unsuccessful?"

Sanchez did not seem intimidated. "Yes, two." Before Dana or Dean could ask further about the unsuccessful operations, Sanchez continued. "No, the subjects did not die. The implants were just too ingrained in their brains to remove without damaging them."

"I see," said Dana.

"Let me warn you now, the procedure is expensive."

"That's not a problem," Dean responded immediately.

"Fine. In fact, we can take a look right now, if you'd like to step over to my scanner."

Dana stood up. "Any cost up front?"

Sanchez smiled. "No, not just to take a look, though I may not really know until I get in there, but it will give me a good idea."

Dana stepped into a holo-imager that was tube-shaped but transparent. Since her entire body was not being scanned, Dr. Sanchez lowered a bowl-shaped object over her head.

"Any radiation from this thing?" Dean asked as he stepped back.

"Not a bit. Now Ms., uh, Captain Stewart, please hold very still."

Dana could see the projection of her brain through the bowl-shaped object in the space in front of her. The doctor paced around it several times, looking closely at different places in the projection—even stepping into the projection at times. Finally, he turned the projector off and the bowl-shaped object retracted from Dana's head.

"You said the power supply implant was at the base of your brain?"

"That's right," Dana said.

"What's wrong?" Dean asked and stepped forward again.

"I thought perhaps the implant might have migrated to another portion of your brain, but I cannot find any evidence of an implant at all. You do still have artificial brain parts, but they are functioning fine without the implant."

Dana was alarmed. Her first thought was they hadn't returned to the correct timeline, but everything else seemed right.

"How could that be?"

Sanchez shook his head. "The only thing I can think of is the implant dissolved somehow. Very rare indeed, but possible."

Chapter 13
The Bad Guys

"What do you mean you lost Dana?" Jump Davis told his two incapable employees.

Slug and Dallas looked at each other. Dallas eyed Slug until he spoke. "Well, she got away before we could catch her. It couldn't be helped," he stammered.

"That's right," said Dallas. "I know where Stewart is headed though. I put a tracking device in her pocket."

"You *saw* her?" Jump asked.

"I bumped into her and her companions at a restaurant here in Reno." Dallas wished they weren't talking to Davis face to face on the screen. He was intimidating and seemed as though he was becoming more and more preoccupied with Stewart all the time. In fact, she wished she could back out of this whole job, but she had already spent some of the money Davis had given her. Plus, he probably wouldn't let her out at this point. She knew too much about him. She knew where two of his three residences were, and she had his private comm number. She also suspected he had a stash of uzerium at one of his residences, although it was probably locked away in a safe or some place out of sight. But what if she and Slug did find Stewart and bring her to Davis? They would no longer be necessary to him, and he might not think anything of getting rid of them permanently. She hadn't thought this out before letting Davis hire her. She was too angry with USSA for not promoting her, and she had taken the job impulsively.

"Well, I couldn't just abduct her with all those people around. And she had her brother, Echo Strand, and some Mexicans with her including a couple of kids. What did you want me to do?"

Jump Davis relaxed a bit. "Okay, you say she flew a private jet to Canada?"

"Yeah, boss," Slug said. "We checked the flight plan."

Jump thought for a moment. "Well, we can't be chasing her all over the continent. She's got to come home eventually. You two go home or wherever you want to go for now. I'll keep a lookout through the cloaked surveillance drones and contact you when I need you again."

Slug and Dallas stood up and looked at Davis for a moment.

"What? You think you'll get more money for *almost* catching her?"

"Oh no, sir," said Dallas.

Davis remained seated at his desk in his Los Angeles office. "Now get out of my sight."

Without a word, Slug and Dallas flipped off the screen, gathered up their belongings, and checked out of their hotel in Reno.

"I'm sure glad Davis didn't ask about Stewart's exact whereabouts," said Dallas.

"What do you mean?"

"Well, she must have found the tracker in flight. I lost her signal before she landed in Vancouver."

"Oh crap," said Slug.

"Yeah, it would have been easy to catch her out in the open if she still had that tracker in her pocket."

"Sure would," said Slug as they strolled down the street. He almost went into a casino, but Dallas grabbed his arm and directed him back to the sidewalk.

"Are you absolutely crazy? How do you think we're going to get back home?"

"I'll win some dough and then we can go." Slug laughed. "Hey, I made a poem!"

Dallas didn't laugh. He had already blown the money he won the night before. "Look, I'm the only one with enough money to get us back to L.A., so you'd better do as I say or be stranded here in this desert town."

"Okay, you're right." He suddenly perked up. "Yeah, we can go scope out Stewart's house in a few days."

"Now you're using your head," said Dallas.

"So how do we get home?"

"Do I have to do all the thinking around here?"

Slug looked thoughtful. "We could hitchhike."

"Oh right, and get mugged?"

"How much money do you have, Dal?"

"Enough." She wasn't going to let on that she had enough for airfare. She wanted to save some for herself to live on for a while when she got back home. In fact, she didn't have a home. She'd have to rent a room somewhere until she got another job or Davis paid them for Stewart. But more and more she was considering ditching the Stewart job and begging USSA for a job, even if it was loading spent nuclear fuel onto droned spacecraft to dump into the sun. That stuff was nasty, and it was still being found all over Earth. She would rather do that than be at the mercy of Davis' wrath. On the base she'd be safe from him. She could live there too, if there were any quarters for rent. Maybe after a few months, she could venture off base and into the city.

"How much?" Slug interrupted her thoughts.

"Enough for the air train. But you're gonna owe me. You understand?" She shook her finger at him.

"Yeah, I know."

Once they were in Los Angeles, Dallas ordered Slug to go check on the Stewart house.

"Ah, way out there? I gotta go home and check on my pad, get some clean clothes, take a shower."

"Well, you do need a shower." Dallas laughed.

"You're not so spic and span yourself," Slug responded.

"Well I have to find a place to live now. I'm going to the base. Ride along with me. I'll pay the taxi fare and you can get off near Stewart's house. I'll give you money to get back home. Do as I say and I won't charge you extra for the fare."

"Okay," Slug conceded reluctantly.

"Contact Davis when you find out something."

"Yes, Ma'am!" Slug saluted.

"C'mon, let's get out of here." The train terminal was crowded and noisy. Dallas was eager to get to the base and find some housing.

When Slug and Dallas parted ways, Dallas focused her mind on how to get out of the deal with Jump Davis. If only she could warn Wilson and Stewart somehow. She'd figure that out later. Now she had to find housing and a job. If USSA didn't take her back, she was in big trouble.

Chapter 14
Eudora Wild

Echo found her mother in a private room on the sixth floor of Mercy General Hospital. A remote monitor stood next to her bed, an oxygen field surrounded her face, indicated by a light blue fog, and one IV drip was inserted into her arm.

Echo took a deep breath as she briskly walked to her mother's bedside. However, she slowed down when she saw her mother appeared to be sleeping. So she quietly pulled up a chair and sat next to her.

While Eudora was sleeping, Echo checked her bank account again. It was too good to be true. She'd have to ask Dean if he deposited money into it, but Dean was still probably off the radar. Echo laughed. Radar wasn't even used anymore, but the expression stuck. Just like "dialing" a comm number, when it was actually punched in or spoken into the device. Then Echo checked her mail—the first chance she'd had since before the trip: 122 messages. She scrolled through them until she found one from Clark, her brother. It was dated yesterday. He told Echo their mother was having chest pains and would probably need medical help.

"Echo, is that you?" Eudora said sleepily.

Echo stood up and leaned over her mother. Her expression was peaceful, but her face was pale. "Mom, I just heard. Are you okay?"

Eudora didn't answer right away. "Yes dear." She reached her arms out to Echo and gently hugged her. Echo didn't resist. She had had her disagreements with her mother, mostly political, but she was happy to see her and glad she was alive.

Echo sat back down. "So, how did it happen?"

Eudora sighed. "Well, I was sitting in my office at the grocery store—oh you must go visit it, Echo. We've got a wide variety of quality goods from all over North America."

"Mom—."

"Oh yes. Well, I was just doing some accounting work when I got a sudden pain in my chest. It was horrible! I've never experienced such pain."

"Well, what did you do?" Echo was impatient for her to get to the point.

"I buzzed Jeremy. He was stocking shelves at the time. I haven't yet earned enough to afford a robotic stocker.

"Mom!"

"Yes, well Jeremy came running in. By that time, I was slumped over my desk. He commed Emergency Services. In the meantime, Jeremy checked my breathing and pulse, which were still active, fortunately. You know, your friend Jeremy was a lifesaver. He's a good worker too. We're planning on putting a deli in the store—should bring in a lot more business. I'm going to ask Jeremy to run it." Her words slowed down and she sounded out of breath.

"Take it easy, Mom. Don't talk too much. Now, how long did it take Emergency Services to get there?"

Eudora took a few breaths before answering. "I don't really know. They said I was unconscious for a few minutes, and my sense of time was distorted. Before I knew it though, I was in the back of an ambulance being transported here. They scanned me and found I had an enlarged heart, so they're growing me a new one.

"How long before it's ready?"

"Nineteen days now they say."

"Good." She wondered if the government would pay for all of this. Organ cloning was expensive, but if Eudora needed help with medical bills, Echo would gladly help out. "Are you comfortable?"

"Yes, a little bored. They don't want me doing any work on my computer. They give me medicine to help me sleep. I guess to help me pass the time."

"Have you had many visitors?"

"Oh yes. Clark even came for a day."

"Yes, I just checked my messages. Nice of them to give him time off."

Eudora's eyes started to close. "You look tired, Mom. I'll come back later."

"Oh, you don't have to go," she said. But a few minutes later she was asleep.

Echo sat at Eudora's bedside for a while, thinking about her relationship with her mother. She had for so long avoided talking to her mother. They differed so much on their political views. Her mother was all for the corporations and didn't like government regulations or handouts. She believed the government wasted money. Echo could agree on part of that, but she basically wanted government regulations. Before the present administration, the corporations had spiraled out of control and merged until there were only three worldwide. The new president had reordered the economy, and Congress went along with it. The new U.S. dollar was backed up by uzerium, land, gold, and other precious metals. The economy was back to 1950s era prices and wages. In a way, it was refreshing. Mid-twentieth century advertising was revived—even in the holo ads. Echo chuckled at the thought of nostalgic ads being displayed in high-tech methods.

But back to her mother. What a scare it was to see her in the hospital, needing a new heart. There was a ninety-four percent success rate of the transplant working, even though it was a clone of the patient's. Would it someday become enlarged like the original heart? She would have to look up statistics on this, or perhaps ask her mother's doctor.

Then she wondered about the cost. She knew there was full government coverage on routine exams and tests, but the patient had to chip in on surgery, cloning, and transplants. If the patient couldn't afford a procedure that was necessary to save her or his life, then the government would pay. Maybe Echo could help pay for some of her mother's medical bills. She would have to inquire about that.

Thinking back, Echo wished she had accepted her mother as she was with all her beliefs. Eudora was Eudora. Why had Echo tried to change her? Echo didn't know why, but it had seemed her mother was prying into her life, asking Echo about her interest in the captain, keeping track of where Echo was, and comming her at inconvenient times. Echo didn't know how to handle this behavior from her mother. She didn't understand some of her own feelings, but she was beginning to understand why she avoided her mother. Now, seeing her here like this, sleeping, her face peaceful, even with the crease permanently etched in the space between her eyes, Echo realized she wanted to spend more time with Eudora, and she would learn how to handle her uncomfortable and untimely inquiries.

Echo left the room and went to the hospital's business office. After her ID verified that she was indeed Eudora Wild's daughter, she finally talked the clerk into telling her how much the hospital bill would be.

"Well, on this, the government will only cover seventy-five percent of the costs—you know the cloning is the most expensive. The organ must be constantly monitored and tested by hospital staff. That takes time and money."

Echo waited anxiously for her to get to the point. "How much?"

The clerk frowned and tapped into his computer. Then he looked up at Echo. "This is just a rough estimate."

"Yes, yes," said Echo impatiently.

"Around five hundred dollars for patient responsibility," said the clerk, looking worried that Echo would object. He was probably used to people raising a fuss over costs.

But Echo was relieved. She was still getting used to this new economy. And with her anonymous bank deposit, she could easily pay the five hundred. "That's great!" Echo blurted out. "Thank you. Thank you." She walked briskly down the long hospital hall and stepped into the elevator.

Chapter 15
Getting Around

Obviously, Echo had a lot to do. Now that Eudora was okay, the next thing on Echo's mind was finding a new place to live, preferably at USSA. She decided to purchase a vehicle. That would make moving much easier.

Once she left the hospital, she hired a ground taxi to take her to vehicle lots. She was surprised you could buy a brand new fully electric car for around four thousand dollars. And that was a vehicle with four seats and a big trunk. At the fourth car lot, she found what she was looking for. It could seat four, but it had two large doors on either side that opened from the bottom up by remote voice command, programmed to the owner's voice. It also had a tracker, which was required by law. If she went to visit Wilson and the captain, she would remove the tracker and leave it at USSA, even though it was illegal to do so. She didn't want to put them in danger by her presence. But if the captain was home, she already was in danger, if Jump Davis or one of his people were still following her. So now she had about fifteen thousand dollars left. She wondered how much apartments were these days and how much USSA housing was. First, she would have to go home and face Sanders.

Echo pulled her vehicle up in front of her apartment building. She parked in a "guest" parking spot. Then she got out of her car and took a long look at its dark blue color and sleek design. The pleasant feeling of owning a vehicle offset her apprehension about talking to Sanders. Echo took her time ascending the steps to her apartment door. She listened at the door and heard footsteps. Then she entered the apartment.

Sanders didn't see her at first. She was folding laundry on the kitchen table. Echo stood near her until she looked up. Her face burst into a smile.

"Echo, you're back!" Sanders dropped her laundry and went over and hugged Echo. Echo hugged her back, but when Sanders tried to kiss her, Echo gently pushed her away.

Sanders frowned. "What's wrong?"

"Let's sit down," said Echo.

Sanders said, "Oh, oh. I know what's coming. Actually, I've suspected it for a long time."

"I'm sorry, Sanders. I do love you, but I'm not in love with you. I wish I were. It's not fair to you for me to stay here."

"To tell you the truth," Sanders said, "I'm not in love with you either. But I think we've grown very close, especially on that trip to the asteroid belt."

Echo sighed relief and nodded. "We did."

"Well, when are you moving out?"

"I have to find a place. I'll move onto the base if there's a place available there. And don't worry, I'll give you money for next month's rent."

"That's very generous of you."

"It's the right thing to do." Echo didn't want to tell Sanders she had acquired a large sum of money, but Sanders would probably find out about her vehicle. She'd tell her about the money eventually.

"So, tell me about your trip. Where's the captain now? Did she get her implant removed?"

"I don't know yet. We parted ways in Reno, and she and her brother took a mini-jet to Vancouver." Then Echo told her the rest of the story while Sanders continued to fold clothes. She told her about the cave, the town called Spike, about Roy Rickerson, and about Reno. But she left out the part about going into an alternate universe. That upset her more than she realized at the time, and she didn't want to talk about it.

After Echo and Sanders had an evening meal, Echo commed the base to inquire about housing. It turned out that only two double units were available. Echo could afford one all to herself, but if someone else needed to move in, she would have to allow it. Those were USSA's rules.

The next day, Echo drove to the base and chose one of the housing units. It had two bedrooms, separated by the common room, so that the roommates would not disturb each other while sleeping. In addition, each bedroom had its own facility. The kitchen was small but had adequate cupboard space. Each bedroom had a full-sized bed, in case a tenant wanted to have company for the night. However, the guest was strictly limited one stay a month at USSA housing, and visitors were screened when they came on base. Echo didn't mind the restrictions—she wasn't planning on having another romantic relationship any time in the near future.

Echo spent most of the day moving her things into her new quarters. The unit was already furnished, so she didn't have to purchase or move any furniture. She chose the bedroom that had a view of the runway, even though it would be noisier. It was brighter and faced west, so that she could see the sunset. The entire unit had central heating and air conditioning. For all this, she paid one hundred dollars a month, with a fifty-dollar deposit.

As the afternoon wound down into evening, Echo finished her activities, opened a cola, and turned on the wallscreen. She hadn't watched more than ten minutes of broadcast news when she heard a knock at the door. She turned down the volume of the news, set down her cola, and cautiously opened the door. Outside stood a tall woman with long curly fiery red hair. She was dressed casually in a USSA sweatshirt and faded blue jeans. She held out her hand to Echo.

"Hi, I'm Dallas Jones, your new roommate."

Chapter 16
Back to L.A.

Dana took an air taxi from LAX to her new house on the outskirts of town, near the USSA base. Her house was located in a developing neighborhood. It was square shaped, tan colored with red trim, and had plenty of land around it—grass, bushes, flowers, and space in the backyard for a vegetable garden. It also had a small greenhouse. The house had two stories plus a daylight basement. It was surrounded on three sides by a two-and-a-half-meter hedge for privacy on the sides and back. She wanted to see out the front—watch for anyone coming to visit or just passing by. Her neighbors on either side were about fifteen or sixteen meters away. This was clearly a luxury neighborhood, as the other houses and those being built, were of the same caliber as Dana's. Two houses were being assembled across the street. Dana was glad to be home. She thought by now, Wilson had erected the force field, but she discovered she could walk right up to the front door. She waved her wristcode across the brass plate on the door, and it swished open.

Walking very softly, she snuck up to Wilson, who was in the kitchen. He was leaning over the sink, rinsing some lettuce and placing it into a small bowl, making himself a salad. She gently reached her arms around his waist and kissed his neck. He smelled clean like he had just taken a shower.

Surprised, he turned around and embraced her. They looked into each other's eyes joyfully, and then they kissed.

Over dinner, she told him about her trip and included the part about going to an alternate universe. She needed to share the story with him—with someone she was close to but who had not had the experience. He did not refute or oppose her story at all. Instead, he was curious, fascinated, and she sensed, a little envious he had not been on the trip and experienced popping in and out of the alternate universe himself. But overall, he seemed relieved to have her back.

Dana got ready for bed. Before splashing water on her face, her palms again began to heat up as they had when she was in the mini-jet, but not as intense this time. She immediately ran cold water over her them, and relief came at once. She didn't mention it to Wilson, who was waiting for her in bed. She was tired of talking, tired of thinking. She wanted to nestle up to him in her own bed.

After making love, Dana went to sleep. She needed more sleep now that she no longer had the implant. Sleep was comforting, healing, and she slept nine straight hours without waking once.

When she woke, Wilson was not in the bed. She lingered for another twenty minutes or more, and then she lazily stretched and climbed out of bed. As she showered and dressed, she thought about what she would do today. They needed to erect the force field for one thing and check for any bugs in or out of the house spying on her. She'd need to hire a bug-sweeper to go over all her electronics and scan the perimeter of her house in all directions for any cloaked devices. She also needed to check in with USSA, which she could do from her home, of course.

Wilson was in the kitchen fixing omelets and toast. When he was finished, he easily slipped an omelet onto each plate, buttered and delivered the toast, and set a container of orange juice on the table.

"Wow, great timing. How did you know I was up?"

"Heard the shower upstairs." Wilson slid into his chair at the table and invited Dana to do the same, pointing with his upturned hand at her chair.

Dana's palms got hot again. This time, she blew on them. The heat receded.

"What's with your hands?" Wilson asked after he poured himself a glass of orange juice. He looked concerned.

"I don't know," she answered. This is the third time it's happened. They got hot all of a sudden."

"You okay now?" Wilson asked.

"Yeah." She frowned in thought, but then went on to enjoy the delicious food Wilson had prepared.

Dana was not accustomed to worrying about things—not for long anyway. Yes, she was a bit stressed commanding that long trip to the asteroid belt. Commanding that huge ship, being responsible for all those people—seventeen miners, eight crewmembers, and one child, not to mention the payload on the way back, and having to check through seven space stations on their way there and back. Going through Customs where registries and cargo were thoroughly inspected added to her stress. These space stations each had their own sovereignty. They could make up their own rules, to a point. For the most part, USSA ships hadn't encountered much trouble through these stations. She'd heard from other captains there had been minor bribes, but they were uncommon. Dana was not going to sign up for any more of those long haul/precious cargo trips for a while, if ever again. Yet, she was glad she had done it. The payment got her this house plus an adequate supply of uzerium.

And then there was Cheyenne. Now Dana was tiring more easily, and she thought about waiting until tomorrow to comm Cheyenne. Again, she was grateful to be back in the universe where she had a daughter. However, she was about one percent unsure she was in the right universe. That gave her enough reason to comm Cheyenne right then.

To Dana's relief, Cheyenne answered and was in a cheerful mood but asked if she could comm back tomorrow. She was right in the middle of editing a movie.

"Sure. Just comm me when you're ready." Dana was relieved Cheyenne answered and glad she wasn't in the chatting mood right then either. Dana just needed to sit down and rest and get used to this new, slower energy in her body. She dropped down in a chair in the common room and closed her eyes. She didn't particularly want to sleep, just rest. Maybe she should see Doc Sereno tomorrow.

Dana sat for what seemed an hour or more in the soft shape-foam chair. Once she stilled herself, she started feeling uncomfortable electricity moving through her face, neck, and head. It didn't hurt, but it was a little unnerving because she didn't know what was happening to her. Instinctively, she put her palms over different parts of her face, neck, and head. Most the time, she placed both hands on parallel spots. Warm energy flowed out of her palms and into her body. Sometimes spots on her head would burn. She'd place a hand there, and the burning energy would dissipate. She'd then shake out her hand, and the hot energy would leave her hand. It felt so good to cup her hands over her temples or her cheeks or jaws. And to place a hand on her forehead and the other on the back of her head. Or to cup her palms over her eyes.

Either her healing abilities had accompanied her from the alternate universe, or anybody could do this and feel better. But she still had a partial artificial brain that was adapting to not having the power implant. Her own energy was powering it now. She was transitioning to this as well.

Chapter 17
Echo's Discovery

Two weeks had passed since Echo had moved into her USSA quarters. Dallas Jones had moved in the very same day. There was something about the woman that looked familiar. Where was her intuition now that she needed it? She didn't seem to have any control over it. The intuition was just there or it wasn't. It'll come to me, Echo told herself.

The captain had commed Echo about ten days ago to let her know she was back. Echo really wanted to go visit her and Wilson right then, but she decided to give them some time alone. The captain's comm call to Echo had to be descrambled too. It was passworded with five, short, rotating passcodes. Echo already had them programmed to try each one until the right one connected. The same method was used from Echo to the captain.

One sunny, cool Saturday morning, Echo decided to comm the captain, but her voicemail answered. So, she decided to drive her new car (minus the tracker) into town and do some shopping. On the way back, she would comm the captain again. But before she did, the captain commed her and told her to come on over.

After they had all said their hellos and hugged, Wilson prepared some tea, and the three of them sat down in the common room.

"So, you're okay?" Echo asked.

The captain shrugged. "A little tired, but I think I'm just feeling how most people feel—needing more sleep than I was getting."

"She's adjusting well to not having an implant," said Wilson.

The captain leaned over and confided in Echo. "The funny thing is, the implant was just gone. It didn't have to be removed."

"She probably left it in the other universe," Wilson said and chuckled. The captain pretended like she was going to hit him, taking her hand and almost slapping him on the back of the head.

"No, I believe her—about the alternate universe," he told Echo. "I've read stories about it happening to other people."

"You'd better believe it," the captain told him. "I've got Strand here to back me up."

"Do you still have your abilities?" Echo asked the captain. She assumed the captain had told Wilson about her healing abilities, but he looked puzzled.

"Oh." She turned to him. "Remember the time my hands got really hot? When I first came home?"

"Yeah, is that still happening?"

"Not so much now, but I've been using my hands to withdraw discomfort from my head and face."

"May I tell him, Captain?"

"Sure."

"In the alternate timeline, I cut my arm on purpose, and put her hand on it. It healed right up."

"No kidding?" Wilson said. "So can you still do it?"

"I don't know. I haven't had occasion to."

Echo pulled out a tiny razor knife and pushed up her sleeve. "We can see right now." But the captain stopped her.

"Oh no you don't. I don't want you hurting yourself again. Once was enough."

"Here, give it to me," said Wilson. But before either Echo or the captain could stop him, he had sliced a tiny cut into his arm.

"Oh, all right."

"Don't you want to know?"

"Yes, but not with either of you hurting yourselves."

The captain placed her palm over Wilson's cut and held it there for about five seconds. When she removed her hand, the bleeding had stopped and there was a scab over the cut.

"Do it again," Echo told the captain. Wilson's expression was curious.

The captain wiped the tiny amount of blood off her hand with her handkerchief, then again she cupped her hand over the wound. She waited about ten seconds this time, then she removed her hand. Echo and the captain peered closely at Wilson's arm. The wound had completely disappeared with no evidence that it had ever been there. There wasn't even a faint scar.

"Incredible," Wilson said and re-examined his arm.

"What about you, Strand?" the captain asked. "Do you still have your abilities?"

Echo thought for a moment, then frowned. "Uh, I don't know. Maybe." And she told them about her sudden urge to contact her mother and finding out she was in the hospital. They inquired about her mother's condition, and Echo told them.

"So, you *do* still have your abilities," Wilson said. "Strong intuition?"

"Yeah, I guess. Did the captain tell you about the bomb on the truck?"

"Yes, she told me."

"Well, I don't know," Echo told both of them. "My new roommate—she seems really familiar, but I just can't place her."

"Do you have a picture of her?" the captain asked.

"Uh, yeah, actually I do." Echo accessed the USSA housing database through her wristcomm and activated a holo of Dallas Jones' face.

The captain studied it for a moment. "She *does* look familiar."

"Not you too," Wilson said.

"No, I—. Let me think." After about twenty seconds, the captain snapped her fingers. "I've got it. She bumped into me at the restaurant in Reno."

"Oh yeah, I saw her getting coffee," said Echo.

"That's not good, Strand. You've got to move out of there or get her to move out."

"I just moved in," Echo protested. "Why?"

"I think she's the reason I ended up with a tracker in my pocket."

"A tracker?" Wilson asked.

"Sorry, I forgot to tell you that part. On the way to Vancouver, I reached into my pocket to get a handkerchief, and I found a small blinking red dot."

"Oh no," said Echo. "She could be working for Jump Davis. Captain, she's going to spy on me no matter where I live. I might as well stay put and keep an eye on her. Maybe I can find out what she's up to."

"She's got a point," said Wilson.

"You just be careful," said the captain.

"I should probably stay away from here," said Echo. "I don't want to endanger you."

"On the contrary," said the captain. "Why don't you bring her over here for dinner?"

The captain seemed fearless, but she was right. No matter the risk, she needed to get to the bottom of this Jump Davis thing. Maybe even confront him.

Echo was excited about finding out what she could about Dallas. She quickly accessed personnel records and discovered Dallas had quit the crew that Wilson was to head up as captain. Then she came back and got a job as a loader. Hmmm.

"Well, I'm going to get back to the base," said Echo.

"I'll comm you a taxi," said Wilson.

Echo broke into a smile, remembering her new vehicle.

"No thanks. Captain and Wilson, come outside. I've got something to show you."

"Nice ride," said Wilson as he looked over the vehicle. "I bet that set you back a bit."

Echo eyed the captain, as she answered Wilson. "Not much. Someone made an anonymous donation to my bank account. Do you know who that might be, Captain?"

She shrugged. "Maybe."

"That was awfully generous of you," Echo said.

"Wish I had a vehicle," Wilson said as he eyed the captain.

"You will, once you command a ship to the asteroid belt for a year." Then she put her arm around Echo's shoulders. "Actually, Dean and I both contributed."

"Well, thank you very much. I can sure use it. I had to move, and the vehicle came in handy."

"So how are things between you and Sanders?"

"Fine. We had dinner. Discussed our relationship. It was my idea to move out, but she was ready to move on too. I hope she's staying with USSA. She's a darned good mechanic. Any idea when we go out again?"

"Haven't heard. I'm sure you can get a ground job in the meantime, if you want to."

"I'll wait a little while. That trip in the truck was a bit rough."

"I know what you mean," said the captain. Wilson was still admiring the vehicle. "Wilson, let's go on in. It's getting cold out here.

"Hey Dana, why don't you get a vehicle?"

"So you can drive it?"

"Of course!"

The captain put her hand on Wilson's back and they walked toward the house. "You're welcome to come back in, Strand," said the captain.

"Thanks. I'm going to head back. I'll comm you about the dinner."

"Okay, Strand. Make it soon," she said.

"Will do. See ya, Captain. See ya, Wilson." Echo waved to them and watched them go into the house. For a moment, she wished she could live there with them. But she dismissed the thought. What would they be, surrogate parents to her? That's the way it felt on the ship. But they weren't on the ship anymore. All of a sudden, Echo felt very lonely. She pushed the emotion down deep, got into her vehicle, and went home to her new quarters she shared with Dallas Jones. Oh boy, this was going to be interesting—taking Dallas to Captain Stewart's house for dinner.

Chapter 18
Dallas' Answer

"No thanks, Strand. I'm not into dinner parties." Dallas was sure that Captain Stewart would recognize her right away. She had to steer clear of her. That might not be so easy if and when the captain came back to the base. She was a sharp one, that Captain Stewart was.

"Ah, c'mon Dallas. I told them I'd bring you over."

"You shouldn't have done that." Dallas went back to watching the wallscreen while Strand continued slouching on the couch, playing with her wristcomm. "How come you're so eager for me to go meet your captain anyway?"

Strand shrugged. "No reason. It's just that she's a pretty interesting woman. And Wilson is fun—and funny. I think we'd have a good time, that's all. If you don't want to go, that's fine. I'll tell them you're not into socializing."

Dallas thought for a moment. "No, don't tell them that. Let me think about this. When's the dinner?"

"Whenever is convenient for all of us. No date has been set. I know you're working, so we can arrange it around your schedule."

"Hmm. I'll let you know before bedtime."

"Sure," said Strand. Her wristcomm chirped. "Oh that's my laundry." She jumped up and went out the door and down the hall to the laundry room.

Dallas kept staring at the broadcast news on the wallscreen, but all the while she was thinking. She could defect on Slug and Jump Davis. It would take a lot of guts on her part. Sooner or later she would run into the captain anyway. And from what she'd seen of her on broadcast, those intense blue eyes could bore right into a person and make them spill the truth. Dallas was terrified when Captain Stewart had gazed at her in the diner. To try and deceive her would be stupid. Besides, she wanted out of the deal with Slug and Davis. On top of that, Slug was a dope. If she did tell all to Strand and Stewart, she would be under their constant scrutiny until she gave them the whereabouts of Jump Davis. Or they might want her to spy on him for them. What a mess she was in.

Strand came back into the room with her folded laundry. After she'd put it away in her bedroom, she went into the kitchen to fix herself a snack. She didn't question Dallas again. A few minutes later, Dallas sat down at the kitchen table across from Strand.

"I've decided to go."

Strand finished eating her bite of toast, then responded. "Good. May I ask what changed your mind?"

"You can ask, but I'll tell you when we're over there for dinner."

Strand raised her eyebrows, but didn't question Dallas further. "Sure. What night is good for you?"

Dallas pretty much knew why she put herself into dangerous or scary situations. It was because of the thrill of it—the adrenaline rush. Dinner would be Saturday evening, and she had two days to get amped up about it. She would visualize the scenario of sitting in Captain Stewart's house—the very house she had broken into—and confessing all. Then she would visualize everyone's response. Would they be angry and throw her out? Would they be shocked and surprised? Maybe, or maybe they already suspected her. Maybe Strand recognized her from the diner and had said something to the others. These thoughts made her heart pound, and she had trouble sleeping. Or maybe they would forgive her, be grateful she had come forth. She would spy for them if they wanted her to; she was certain of it. She would have a relieved conscience too. But she did have an ulterior motive—maybe she could get her job back with her old crew, now that Coop Wilson was in command.

After several hours of tossing and turning, Dallas' body took over and relaxed into sleep. She awoke to her alarm much too early at 0600.

Still a bit groggy from sleep, Dallas rode the USSA bus out to the desert to begin a long day of loading canisters of nuclear waste into a rocket. She, among nine other workers, donned radiation suits while they operated lifters and loaders. Fortunately, the suits were air-conditioned. Although it was almost winter, it still got hot out in the desert during the day. The work was drudgery, even though the machines did most the work. The pay was good, but she still wanted desperately to get back on a flight crew, preferably the one she'd left. She really didn't want to familiarize herself with a brand new set of crewmembers. But she would if she had to.

The time went by slowly. There were so many canisters. About the time nuclear fusion reactors were invented, the solar power satellites became operational. Now, nuclear power plants were obsolete, but the fission reactors sure left a lot of waste over the last 175 years. It was necessary to get rid of the waste, as some of the canisters were leaking. Every week, a gigantic rocket was launched from the desert, its propulsion boosters falling into the Pacific Ocean to be re-used.

The crew got two half-hour breaks and an hour for lunch. But it took about fifteen minutes to climb in and out of the suits. Some people skipped that part and took their breaks in the radiation shack, just so they could sit down longer. But for lunch, they all removed their suits. This was the only time Dallas sat down with the entire team. No one lasted very long at the job, and Dallas was told that at least one new person came on board every week. She had been there for almost three weeks, and now she was ready to quit too. What kept her going was thinking about the upcoming dinner at Captain Stewart's house. If she was lucky, she would be able to quit this job next week.

Chapter 19
Eudora Gets a Heart

Echo watched the live video feed of her mother's surgery from a small private room just off the main waiting room. At first, she was afraid to see her mother's chest being opened. But as she watched, she became fascinated as a team of skilled surgeons carefully removed her enlarged heart and replaced it with her new cloned heart. The doctor had explained to her that the heart had become enlarged because it had trouble pumping enough blood into her system. Her mother had congestive heart failure and didn't even know it. Her blood pressure was also too high, and these conditions had led to an enlarged heart.

The surgery lasted three and a half hours, but Echo stayed and watched the whole thing. Once she got up to purchase a cola from the machine in the lobby and once to use the facility. When the surgery was over, she waited nervously in the lobby for the doctor to come out. When she finally did, she told Echo that the surgery had gone well and that her mother was still asleep. She told Echo to go home and come back in the morning. Echo thanked the doctor and commed Clark, leaving a voicemail telling him their mother's surgery was a success and that she would keep him updated.

As Echo left the hospital, she felt a sense of relief. She'd had her differences with her mother, but she certainly didn't want to lose her. She hoped she could sleep tonight.

That evening, Echo talked to Dallas about her mother's surgery.

"I don't think I could have watched," Dallas said.

"I was scared to at first, but after I started watching, I couldn't stop."

"Is she going to recover okay?" Dallas asked. She seemed sincerely interested.

"The doctor said the chances are good." Echo blocked out any thoughts that something could go wrong during her mother's recovery.

"I'm glad." Dallas was still in her work clothes, a poly denim jumpsuit with a USSA logo on the front pocket. And she had cut her beautiful red hair into a short bob, but the wave in her hair framed her face in a way that made her look younger than her thirty-five years.

"Tough job, that loading," Echo said. "I guess short hair makes it easier to wear your gear."

Dallas fluffed her hair, still getting used to it, Echo assumed. "Yeah, it was what I could get."

"I did loading for a while—not nuclear waste."

"Yeah, where'd you work?"

"Here on the base. It got so hot in the warehouse, I passed out."

"Well, our suits are air conditioned—that's one good thing."

Echo wanted to ask her how long she thought she'd last on the job, but she thought it might be offensive or impolite. She was getting to know Dallas, and for the most part, liked her well enough. She didn't talk a whole lot, minded her own business, and was agreeable. Echo was comfortable around her and now questioned her own motives for asking her to dinner at the captain's house.

The next day, Echo drove to the hospital. When she entered the room, her mother was sitting up in bed, having breakfast. Echo was relieved. Eudora was strong and motivated. The hard part of her recovery would probably be getting her to take it easy.

"Mom, how are you doing?"

"Echo, come over here." Eudora motioned with her hand. She was wearing a hospital gown that fastened in the back, so Echo was unable to peek at her chest. However, the doctor had reassured her that Eudora would not have a scar, and that the breastbone would heal completely because of the fusion techniques applied to it before they lasered her skin back up.

"How long do you have to stay in the hospital?"

"Oh, I'm not sure. I hope only a couple of days. Jeremy is running the store by himself."

Echo sat down next to the bed. "I hope you don't overdo yourself. The doctor says you need to take it easy."

"Oh, I will, dear. Would you do me a big favor and go check on the store? I've been in touch with Jeremy, and he says he could use some help. Do you suppose you could go over there and give him a hand? Even a few hours would help."

"Sure, Mom. I'd like to see Jeremy anyway. I can go this afternoon."

"Thank you, dear." Eudora patted Echo's shoulder.

"The doctor says you won't have a scar."

Eudora peeked down her gown. "It's barely noticeable now. I hope they're right."

"I'm glad."

"Echo, how long since you've had a physical exam?"

"Oh, I had one a little over a year ago, just before we went on our long space journey."

"Well, you should have one every year. I put it off, and this is what happened to me. Promise you'll make an appointment."

"I will. USSA requires it anyway."

"Are you going back to work?"

"I have some furlough time left, but I'll have to get a physical before going back to work." Echo hoped her mother didn't ask about her finances.

Eudora finished her breakfast and pushed the tray aside. At least she had a good appetite, Echo thought.

"I've got to go, Mom."

"Can you come back tonight?"

"Can't. I have a dinner to go to."

"Oh? Where?"

"At the captain's. I'm taking my new roommate." Echo stood up and headed for the door before her mother could question her any further. "Bye, Mom. I'll comm you later."

"Okay, dear." Eudora slid down into her bed, lowering the back of it so she could lie down.

On her way out, Echo stopped at the administration office and put five hundred dollars onto her mother's bill. Then she was off to her mother's grocery store.

Chapter 20
The Store

Echo found a spot in the small parking lot of her mother's grocery store. Previous to the new economy, people could only shop electronically or go to a big warehouse. The grocery stores of the twentieth-first century were rare because they did not turn a profit. But now, in the post-corporate monster world, smaller stores were popping up. Echo's mother was smart enough to foresee an economic opportunity and the future of the grocery store.

Echo found Jeremy in the office above the store with a lookout window. She climbed the rickety plastiwood stairs, holding on to the wobbly handrail. This building was old. He was busy with three transparent displays. It looked as though he were writing things down on used paper. Echo glanced to the right of his desk. There was a stack of assorted papers—printer paper, tissue paper, and packing paper. And beside that were some smaller pieces for making notes. He also had a roll of newsprint (without the print). No one had seen printed newspapers for almost a hundred years, except in museums. In the last century, she'd been told, it was often used to wrap fish.

Jeremy caught Echo in his peripheral vision then turned to face her. He looked happily surprised. Jeremy stood up and reached out to embrace her. "Hey, Echo!"

She embraced him back, warmly. Then they pulled away and looked at each other, each of them glad to see an old friend. "Eudora wanted me to stop here and give you a hand. Said you were really swamped."

"How is your mom doing?"

"Good. She's told me she commed you several times."

"Well, you just saw her in person. It's sometimes hard to tell how a person is over the comm's vid."

"She's good—her color is good, but I think she may want to come back to work too soon."

"Yeah, I could really use some help."

"Can you afford to hire another employee?"

"Barely, but business is picking up all the time. That's why I'm so busy. The store is growing. People are buying like mad, plus, they're requesting items we don't have, so I have to order them."

Echo noticed when she walked into the store that it was full of busy shoppers. It had glass doors and faux marble floors, a composite that was smooth but as hard as granite. The building had once been one of NorCom's storage houses—not as big as one of their standard warehouses where people shopped. This structure had been an armory. Plus, it was where uniforms were kept for the corporate soldiers. When the government, with the help of the Resistance, won the war with NorCom, this place became government property and was put up for sale.

Shelves along the aisles were low—about Echo's height, several inches shorter than the captain, but Echo could see that some had been added onto. Freezers and refrigerators were against one wall, and a small amount of general merchandise was separated from the food.

"I can help you for only a few hours today, Jeremy. I'm taking my new roommate to the captain's house dinner tonight."

Jeremy raised his eyebrows. "You broke up with Sanders?"

"Yeah. I moved back into base housing."

"So is this new roommate more than just a roommate?"

"No." Echo sensed Jeremy was interested in dating her. They'd been best friends for years, but Echo's intuition told her Jeremy wanted more than friendship. "I'm just not into having a relationship right now."

"Sure," he said without expression.

"Anyway, the captain's suspicious of her. Thought she saw her in Reno. I saw her too, getting coffee at a diner. The captain claims she dropped a tracker in her pocket. I didn't see that." Echo wondered if she was telling too much. Jeremy already knew about Echo's trip and the break-in at the captain's house, and that Jump Davis was trying to capture the captain.

"So, the captain wants to pump her for information," Jeremy stated as if it were obvious.

Echo sighed. "Yeah, I guess. I'm curious—very curious—as to what will happen tonight. Yet, I've gotten to know Dallas over the past few weeks, and she seems pretty sincere. I hope she wants to go along with whatever the captain has in mind."

"Just be careful. She is living with you and could rip you off."

"Yeah, but I don't have a whole lot in those quarters—there isn't room for much. And I don't have jewelry, or wads of cash laying around."

"Well, I guess you know what you're doing."

Echo removed her jacket and hung it on a discolored hook in the corner of the office. She walked briskly back to Jeremy's desk and stuffed her hands in her jeans pockets. "So, what would you like me to do?"

"I could use help out on the floor."

Echo remembered seeing several people in green grocery aprons, two overseeing the self-checkout, and two others stocking shelves. "Stocking shelves?"

"Yeah. See that guy with the black and white marbled hairdo?" Jeremy pointed out the office window to a person removing cans from a crate and putting them onto the shelf.

Echo nodded.

"That's Marko. Go introduce yourself and tell him you're there to help for a few hours. He's got a lot of work to do."

"I'm not going to be mopping the floor, am I?"

"If he needs you to—if there's a spill."

She looked at him for a second.

"Well, you offered to help."

"I know." Echo exited the office, tapped down the stairs, and found Marko.

Chapter 21
The Dinner

"This is a pretty stylish vehicle, Strand," Dallas said.

"Thank you. I'm still getting used to driving it."

"Why don't you put it on auto?"

"I enjoy being in control, my hands on the steering wheel, my feet on the pedals."

Dallas watched as Strand drove off the base and through residential streets. "How far to Captain Stewart's house?" She was becoming more nervous the closer they got. She knew exactly where the house was, having broken into it. She was also hoping the captain might not recognize her with her short hair.

"Oh, about three and a half kilometers after exiting the base." Strand turned her head and looked at Dallas for a moment while they were at a stop signal. Was she somehow aware of Dallas' past? A robotic male voice came through the car's speakers alerting the stop several seconds before the stop sign appeared.

"You suppose I could drive it some time?"

"Uh, well I don't know if my insurance covers other drivers.

"We could drive it in the parking lot on the base."

Strand hesitated. "Maybe. We'll see."

"That would be great. I've driven motorcycles, but I don't currently have one."

All too soon, they pulled up into the circular driveway. Dallas noticed several small red lights floating in the air in front of the house. They've installed a force field, she thought.

Echo commed the house. "We're here," she said. In a few seconds, the small red lights turned to green. The two women walked to the front door. As soon as they were in front of it, the door slid open. Coop Wilson stood in the doorway with a smile on his face.

"Welcome," he said, and waved his arm toward the inside.

Dallas tried not to look like she was in awe of her surroundings, but she couldn't help gawking at the interior of the spacious house.

Wilson led them into the common room and invited them to be seated on the couch.

"Would you like something to drink?" Wilson asked. "We have soda, beer, wine, water, orange juice."

"I'll take a cola if you have one," Strand said.

"I'll have a beer," said Dallas, thinking it might relax her.

"Be right back," said Wilson.

Dallas caught herself holding her breath, knowing Captain Stewart could enter the room at any moment.

Several minutes later, Wilson and Stewart came back with their drinks on a tray. Wilson placed a beer on the table next to his chair and an orange juice on the table next to Stewart's chair as she sat down. He handed Strand her cola and Dallas her beer already poured into a glass. Dallas made herself look Stewart in the eye. Stewart briefly acknowledged Dallas, but didn't let on that she recognized her. Dallas relaxed.

Captain Stewart wore a dark blue, well-fitted pair of blue jeans and white sneakers. For a top, she wore a white blouse with a tan blazer. Although a little tired looking, she was fit and trim. Wilson wore a tan pair of slacks and a royal blue USSA T-shirt. Dallas and Strand were also dressed casually, but neat and clean. Strand wore a snug fitting light blue jumpsuit with a black leather jacket. Dallas wore a black pair of jeans with a light blue T-shirt over which she wore a black zip-up hooded sweatshirt.

"You were on my crew," Wilson said to Dallas, getting right to the point. "What made you leave?" He asked the question casually as if he were asking someone where they bought an article of clothing, but Dallas' heart pounded. She might as well tell the truth.

"To tell you the truth, Captain Wilson, I was hoping to be promoted to captain or at least first officer, but I was passed over. Looks like you were the lucky one."

"Please call me Wilson. Yes, I applied and got the job."

Dallas took a gulp of her beer. "Well, we all can't be captains," she said without malice. "I'm sure the board weighed everyone's qualifications." Dallas was trying to convince herself. No one asked what she was doing now. Strand must have informed them of her unpleasant job.

"Well, if anyone is hungry, why don't we go into the dining room. I hope you like Italian," Stewart said to Dallas.

Dallas couldn't remember the last time she had any Italian food, except the occasional spaghetti and meatballs from a can. She wasn't into cooking, and normally ate convenience foods. "Oh, I like about anything," Dallas said.

The four of them sat at a small oval dining room table with a red and white checkered tablecloth, in the Italian restaurant tradition. Several large dishes of food were already on the table. Wilson sat at one end of the table and Captain Stewart at the other. Strand sat at a ninety-degree angle to them, and Dallas sat across from her. Dallas finished her beer.

"Another brew?" Wilson asked her.

"Maybe later. Thank you."

Captain Stewart served herself some salad then passed the bowl to Dallas. The Caesar salad was tossed with dressing, croutons, and Parmesan cheese. Dallas took a healthy serving. The next platter contained an assortment of meat, cheese, and marinated vegetables. And the main dishes were meat-filled tortellini and cheese ravioli. Dallas took a serving of each. She waited until everyone had served themselves.

"Go ahead and dig in," said Captain Stewart as she stabbed her fork into her salad.

Dallas tried not to eat too fast, but the food was so good, she had to control herself. The conversation centered around the house, its furnishings and the recently erected force field.

"We had a break-in a while back," Wilson said.

Dallas acted surprised. "That's terrible. Did they get anything?"

Strand spoke up. "No, fortunately Wilson and I were here and fended them off."

Dallas was glad she and Slug had worn full-face masks. "How many were there?" Dallas asked.

"Two," said Wilson. "They were after Dana."

"They grabbed me, but I managed to get away from them," said Captain Stewart.

"What did they want with you?"

"Someone from my past is after me."

Dallas didn't inquire any further. Once they had finished eating, Captain Stewart asked if anyone wanted dessert. Dallas thought she could hold a little more, but she waited to see if anyone else spoke up first.

"Sure, what is it?" Strand asked.

"Spumoni," said Captain Stewart.

Dallas didn't know what that was, but she decided to try it. It wasn't every day a person got an elaborate dinner.

Captain Stewart went into the kitchen and came out with a tray of dishes filled with what looked like multicolored ice cream. She went around the table and set a dish at each person's place. Then she set the tray aside and sat down. Everyone waited for her to take a bite of the dessert first. Dallas inspected it, then took a small spoonful. It was delicious.

"Umm. This is great. Did you make it?"

Captain Stewart laughed. "Hardly."

"The entire dinner was catered," said Wilson. "We can't take the credit for any of the preparation."

"Well, it was all very good," Dallas said. "I don't think I'll have room for another beer."

"Yes, it's delicious," said Strand. "So what's the occasion?"

Occasion? Didn't Strand know? What occasion? Dallas thought.

Captain Stewart looked at Dallas with her intense blue eyes just as Dallas was swallowing the last bite of her ice cream filled with pieces of fruit and nuts and whipped cream. "We need your help, Dallas," she said.

Dallas almost choked. She felt her face flush. The ice cream stuck in her throat, but she managed to finally swallow it. Then her stomach with all that food in it, churned into a big knot. Her heart pounded, but after all that, she managed to respond.

"*My* help?"

"Relax," said Stewart. "I recognize you. You must remember dropping that tracker into my pocket in Reno."

Dallas didn't try to deny it. Stewart was sharp. "Please accept my apology, Captain. I wouldn't do it now."

"How can I be sure of that?" Stewart said sternly.

"Will you excuse me, please?" I need to use the facility."

Wilson stood up. "I'll show you where it is."

Dallas barely noticed the purple and white décor, the white bathtub/ shower combo, and the quaint sink with brass water faucet plumbing. She lifted the toilet lid and leaned over, but nothing would come up. She took a few deep breaths and composed herself. Then she flushed the toilet to make it sound as if she used it in case Wilson was standing outside the door waiting for her. The knot in her stomach eased only slightly. She took one look in the mirror and told herself she could do this. Anyway, the captain asked for her help. She and Wilson must trust her. How could they though? She wasn't going to let on that she was one of the people who had broken into the house—that she would keep to herself.

When Dallas came out of the facility, Wilson *was* standing there. So much for trust, she thought. They were going to keep a close eye on her. She wondered if Strand knew what this dinner was all about beforehand. Probably.

Everyone was back in the common room. Captain Stewart was sitting on the couch by herself. "How are you feeling?"

Dallas was honest. "Not so good," she said as she put her hand on her stomach.

"Come over here next to me," Captain Stewart said.

Dallas sat down on the couch and the captain turned toward her. "Just lean forward a little."

Dallas did as she was told. Then the captain placed one hand on her stomach and the other on her back. Her hands were warm. Dallas relaxed. She hadn't been touched in a long time, and it was comforting. "What are you doing?"

"Just breathe naturally," the captain said.

Dallas didn't argue. She was starting to feel better. The knot was dissolving, and she was beginning to digest her food. After several minutes, the captain removed her hands.

"Better?"

"Yes, thank you."

"All right. Strand says we can trust you. Is she right?"

Dallas took a deep breath and let it out. She looked at Strand and then at Wilson. They were sitting in chairs across from her.

"Yes, I think I know what you want, and I will help you."

"Okay," said the captain. "Here's what we would like you to do."

Chapter 22
Davis Enterprises

Jump Davis sat at his wide desk in a large office on the forty-ninth floor of a fifty-two-story silver and glass building in the business district of Los Angeles. On the walls were framed photographs. One was of a USSA TC-Twilight 440 spaceplane with its body in the exosphere and its nose just touching the black of space. Another was a popular make and brand of vehicle, red and sleek. And another, an almost human-looking male robot. These were products for which his company made artificial intelligence parts. With his uzerium mine on Mars, he had been able to get a head start on his business after the U.S. president reset the economy. The only downside was that the precious ore was expensive to ship to Earth. However, he was doing fine for now. He had everything he wanted except for Dana Stewart. He felt possessive and angry and helpless in that department. Once in a while he felt a pang of love for her, but he would chastise himself for thinking of her that way. He was so angry that she broke up with him that he was unable to feel love. Where were his people anyway?

Davis dialed Slug Spillman's number. He gave Slug and Dallas new comms every week, delivered by a courier. But he hadn't heard back from either of them in over a week.

Slug answered right away. "Oh, uh, I'm back here in L.A. Dallas, she's back in town too, but she took off." Slug's miniature holo popped up on Jump's desk.

"How long since you talked to her?"

"Um, actually, I talked to her last night. She should be contacting you soon. She's got some information for you, she said."

"I want both of you in my office tomorrow morning."

"What time?"

"Give me a second." Jump vocally ordered his schedule for November. A blue display appeared in the air. He had a 9:30 available. He confirmed with Slug. "You get a hold of her and bring her, you hear?"

"Yes, boss. Nine-thirty. We'll be there." The holo of Slug disappeared.

"Your ten-thirty is here," a female robot voice announced.

"Thank you, Wanda. Send him in." Jump's schedule was fairly busy with current and potential clients.

Once noon came, he stepped out of his office and surveyed his employees' large office. He didn't like barriers between or around their desks. He wanted to see across the entire office. The thirty-two desks were separated by enough space that workers were able to maintain a modicum of privacy and hear themselves on their comms. Each desk also had one or two extra chairs for clients and visitors. Some people were leaving for lunch. He let them take lunch whenever they wanted as long as there were at least two people in the office at all times. Manufacturing was done on the floor below—more expensive in a tall building than a warehouse, but Jump could afford it. He wanted to have easy access to the products as well as be able to take potential clients on a tour of the factory. In fact, he thought he'd go down there now. Most would be out for lunch, but a few still might be there taking their lunch in the staff room.

Jump wandered through the clean factory, stopping briefly to say hello to two technicians who were still working on a project. The area looked more like a laboratory than a factory, being part research and development and part production. Jump wandered until he reached an unmarked door. Marking the door as private would just make people curious. He punched in the key code, the door slid up, and he stepped inside, making sure no one saw him. The lights automatically came on, but the door was solid and sealed all the way around so no one could see any light escape to the outside. Then he lifted the sheet from his secret project.

He had copied the design from another human robot, but he'd modified the shape. It was still all wires and tiny circuit boards; he wouldn't put the skin on until the brain was finished. He pulled a holo generator from his pocket and activated several displays of Dana. He was able to strip the layers of clothing from her by a few simple computer commands. Then he overlaid the holo onto the android skeleton to make sure the skeleton was the right shape. Every time he added hardware and components to the android, its shape changed slightly. With a few more computer commands, he was able to stretch or compress the skeleton so that it matched the hologram.

After a few adjustments and stopping to admire his work, Jump checked his watch. The lunch crowd would be returning soon. With his one-way cameras inside the room, he was able to see if anyone was in his line of sight before coming out the door. He covered his android again and double-checked the cameras. No one was in sight. Then he quickly opened the door and slipped out. As far as he knew, only one person had seen him just after he was out the door when it was already closed. That was a woman technician named Mabel, about three weeks ago, but he suspected she had no idea what he was doing standing outside the door. Normally, he worked on the project after hours when no one was around, but today he couldn't help peeking at it. Besides, there was a kind of thrill about sneaking around like this, even if this was his own company.

Back in his office, Jump removed his lunch from the refrigerator. He had a ham sandwich and an apple he had had delivered from a deli earlier that day. While he ate, he activated his monitors to make sure all his employees were back at work. Then he remotely locked his office door and admired holos of Dana. He was fidgety—eager to see Slug and Dallas—but afraid they'd lost Dana's trail. But Slug had said Dallas had some information, so that was promising. He could hardly wait.

Chapter 23
Dana's Plan

"How do you know you can trust this Dallas woman?" Wilson asked Dana as they were sitting at the breakfast table.

"I don't, but Strand has pretty good instincts about her. Anyway, it doesn't matter if she betrays us. All we want is for her to bring Jump to me."

"Entrapment," Wilson said, as he rubbed his hands together.

"That's right. We are setting a trap."

"What if he refuses to meet you?"

"That's a possibility. Then I'll figure something else out."

"This sounds pretty dangerous to me, Dana, letting him abduct you."

"I can take care of myself. Of course I'll have help. I'm counting on you, Strand, and the others."

Wilson took a sip of his coffee. "I don't like this, but you've got your mind set on it and there isn't anything I can do to stop you."

"That's right. I've got an appointment at two-fifteen today with Doc Sereno to get the subcutaneous tracker implanted."

"That'll be interesting. Davis will never think to look for it in your foot, but what if he scans you and finds it?"

It's a chance I'm willing to take." Dana finished her coffee and put her mug in the sink. "Besides, he's not going to get very far. Once he nabs me, you and Strand will call in the crew. And hopefully, it'll be caught on the van's cameras. That's the plan." Dana slumped down in the kitchen chair. "Whew, all of a sudden I'm exhausted."

"Go take a nap."

"I'm not used to being tired so much. Sure hope I snap out of this." Living without the implant was quite an adjustment to make to her metabolism. She wasn't used to feeling tired so much, and she wasn't used to worrying about things. She wasn't really worried about the Jump Davis abduction—they would get him—but she was a bit concerned about her physical health. Before, she took it for granted that her body would perform for her. Now, she had to take at least two naps a day. Who knew when she would be ready for a space flight again?

"Sorry, Captain, I can't tell you for sure that you'll have more energy in the future. But the body adapts, and I believe you will."

Dana slipped off the exam table and quickly changed the medical gown for her jumpsuit, while Doc Sereno made notes in her file. Then he turned toward her.

"I'm ordering a head scan for you. You can go do it now. I'll get you the results and my comments in a few minutes. Have you been exercising?"

"No, not much."

"I recommend you go to the gym. Brush up on your martial arts. Don't overdo it. Maybe a half hour at a time at first. Your blood pressure and weight are good."

"Okay, Doc." Dana slipped on her shoes and her silver USSA jacket. Might as well get this over with, she thought. She wasn't too worried. She'd had a head scan in Vancouver recently. Wouldn't Doctor Sanchez have said something if he saw anything unusual in her head?

Dana strode down the hallway of the clinic, took a right, and then another right to the reception desk. She told the receptionist why she was there, then took a seat and waited. No one else was waiting. In a few minutes, a short man in a white lab coat ushered her into the scanning room.

"Not much radiation with these scans, so don't worry. Please have a seat right here, Captain Stewart."

She sat on a utilitarian black chair.

"Okay, be very still," said the technician.

Dana took a deep breath. A white bowl-shaped image of light lowered over her head. She could see through its translucent fog.

"Still now." She heard a click. "Okay, done."

The holographic image would be transferred to Doc Sereno. As she headed for the door, her comm beeped. "All okay with the head scan, Doc Sereno's voice came through. Do you want to see it?"

Dana felt relief. "Nope, no need, Doc. Thanks."

While here at the base, she decided to go to Scheduling. Maybe they had more information than she could get remotely, and she found out they did. Good. She was eager to get back out in space.

Back home she took a nap then showered and dressed for company. After dinner, they started showing up. Tommy TwoTrees, her navigator, Bugs Anderson, her engineer, Marg Mackovich, her freight coordinator, and of course, Echo Strand, her young systems tech. Doc Sereno was part of her crew as well, but she didn't need him for her plan. Dana's crew hadn't been assigned a new XO yet.

"Hi everyone, thanks for coming. I know I can trust you all with this, but it is strictly volunteer."

TwoTrees raised his slim brown arm. She nodded at him like a teacher would in a classroom. "I thought you were going to announce a space flight."

"I have some news on that front too, but first I need your help with something."

They listened as she explained her plan to catch Jump Davis in the act of abducting her from Fleming's Steakhouse downtown.

"What if he has more people with him than we have?" asked the brazen Mackovich without raising her hand, which wasn't necessary anyway.

Dana shrugged. "Well, there's where we hope we can trust Dallas Jones to let us know how this is going to go down."

"And what if they *do* have more people and firepower than we do?" asked Bugs Anderson. "You might find out too late to do anything about it."

"That's where we take a chance. Listen, I know this plan has some danger, but I have to get this guy off my back. I can't go running off to escape him all the time."

"Well, I'm in all the way," said Strand. The others didn't hesitate to volunteer.

"Okay." Dana clapped her hands together. "We'll make this operation go as smoothly as possible."

"Just like we did on the moon when NorCom took over the lunar base," said Mackovich. The others nodded.

"Now, I checked with Scheduling this afternoon and found out we've got a trip to Mars eight weeks from now. This info isn't public yet, so try and keep it under your hats. Plus, there could be changes, delays, or even a cancellation in the meantime, so don't get your hopes up."

Strand nodded once. "So it's the same as last time? A passenger and cargo haul and uzerium pickup?" She didn't seem very enthusiastic.

"No passengers, just cargo," said Dana.

TwoTrees said nothing, but Dana could tell by his facial expression that he was pleased. Same with the others except for Strand. She wondered why. The others wanted to get back out there—do their real jobs. There was a general mumble among the group.

"I can't even tell you when the word will be official. Probably a few days before the flight," said Dana. "Of course we'll start checking and loading right after we hear. Now, everybody have some refreshments."

Chapter 24
Dallas Faces Davis

Dallas and Slug stood in front of Jump Davis' desk in his luxurious office.

"Sit down," he motioned with his hand.

They nervously took a seat in front of his desk.

"Now, you've been in my employ for almost two months. I gave each of you a three thousand dollar advance, but I'm seeing no results." His voice was calm, but Dallas could sense the anger within and that he was struggling to control himself.

"Sorry boss," said Slug. "I have your money." Evidently he'd found someone to lend him the money or else he'd robbed someone.

Davis stood up and pounded his desk with his fist. "I don't want the money! I want Dana Stewart!" Then he looked at Dallas. "And you two better figure out how to catch her." He sat back down, calming himself once again.

"Yes boss," said Slug.

Dallas cleared her throat.

"You have something to say?" he said to her abruptly.

"I've seen . . ." she stopped herself from saying Stewart. "I've been in contact with Echo Strand."

"Been in contact?" Slug laughed. "You live with her." Dallas frowned at him. She didn't want Davis to know how close she'd gotten to Strand. He might think she had turned on him

"Is this true, Dallas? You live with Strand?"

"It was by accident, sir. You see, I got this job at the USSA base and they partnered me up in base housing with her. It was the only available place to stay."

Davis seemed pleased. "Well, this is to our advantage. Certainly you can get your foot in the door, literally, with Stewart. Now we can make a plan."

"Mr. Davis, sir, there already is a plan."

Slug and Davis both looked surprised. "Why didn't you tell *me?*" Slug accused as he pointed his finger into his chest.

"Take it easy. I just found out," she told him. Then she turned to Davis. "It just so happens that Stewart wants you to meet her at Fleming's Steakhouse downtown for lunch."

Davis frowned and was silent for a moment. "She's up to something."

"Maybe she just wants to talk—work out something reasonable with you," Dallas said.

"She wants me to stop pursuing her, but talk isn't going to make that happen."

Dallas knew he was jonesing for her in a bad way and couldn't resist the offer. Davis stood up and paced back and forth behind his desk, the tip of his thumbnail in his mouth. "Let me think about this." A few minutes went by, then he said, "She probably wants to catch me in the act of kidnapping her." He clapped his hands together, and Dallas gulped. He figured that out fast, she thought.

"We could get her after you leave the restaurant. Take her to a secluded alley," Dallas suggested.

Davis sat down again. "I'm sure she has a plan for that too." Then he looked up at both of them. "Let me get back to you on this." Then, looking at Dallas, he said, "Tell her I accept. Get a time and date. "I'll figure out a plan in the meantime. And neither of you leave town. I'll need your help. Now, get out of here. I'll be in touch."

Dallas felt like a double agent. On the one hand, she'd get the rest of the money Davis had promised her if she helped kidnap Stewart; on the other hand, Coop Wilson might place her on his crew if she helped Stewart, but then she'd have to pay Jump back the three thousand. Of course, if she betrayed him, he would be after her anyway. Not if he was in prison though.

According to Stewart's plan, Dallas would have to pretend to help abduct her anyway. In fact, Stewart wanted Davis to kidnap her with Dallas along, recording the entire event with a special hidden camera enmeshed in her clothing. It was a dangerous plan for Stewart, but as Dallas was learning, Stewart wasn't afraid of danger.

Chapter 25
Echo's Quest

While Echo was waiting around to hear from the captain about when the Jump Davis plan was going to go down, she grew restless. She didn't feel like working in the warehouse at USSA, and she had enough money to tide her over for at least six months.

Echo drove out to her mother's store and was shocked to find her mother sitting in the office so soon after getting out of the hospital.

"I'm fine, really," Eudora said. She was sitting at the desk where Jeremy had been the last time Echo visited the store. However, she didn't seem to be stressing herself. She had a few papers in front of her, but mostly she was looking out the office window down on the floor. She was in her element, comfortable owning a profitable business.

"I came to find out about a job."

"For yourself?" Eudora seemed surprised.

"Yes, just a temporary one."

"Hmm," said Eudora and looked thoughtful. "The pay won't be high. I can't afford the government minimum wage accorded food workers. I'd make a better profit if it weren't for that stipulation from the president."

"That's okay. You don't have to pay me."

"That's very generous of you, Echo. Why the sudden interest in helping me out?"

Echo didn't really want to tell her mother she wanted to keep an eye on her, but that's exactly what she wanted to do. She knew that having a heart transplant wasn't a guarantee of avoiding another heart-related illness. Eudora tended to work herself too hard, and Echo didn't want Eudora to relapse. "I need something to keep me busy until I get called to a flight," Echo said.

"So how long will that be?"

"I'm not sure," said Echo. It's supposed to be about seven weeks from now, but that could change. The government isn't doing too well financially, but it does need the uzerium from Mars."

"Well, I'm fine as long as they don't raise my business taxes."

Echo shrugged. "You know, the president wants our currency backed up by precious ore, but I can't tell you what they'll do regarding the taxes."

"That's an understatement." Eudora didn't like the new socialistic government, but Echo didn't want to get into a political discussion with her. It always ended in an argument.

"So, when can I start?"

"Tomorrow, if you'd like."

Eudora looked up a file on her computer and found a choice of schedules for her daughter. Echo looked them over. "How about early mornings? I like the six to two shift."

Eudora turned to her. "Then you'd have to get up pretty early to catch the train."

"That's okay." Echo didn't think she'd drive her vehicle to work. She still didn't want Eudora to know about it. If she told her, then Eudora would fire a string of questions at her as to how and why she got the money for it. Echo didn't want to go into the story of her trip to the mountains with Captain Stewart and the others. However, she kept having dreams about the cave.

"By the way, my hospital bill was paid anonymously. Do you know anything about that?"

"No, but that's wonderful," said Echo. She hoped her mother didn't detect her lie. She decided to leave before Eudora could ask any more questions. "I'll see you tomorrow, Mom."

The next day, Echo began her work by moving palettes. There were so many palettes of items to be unloaded, there was not enough room for them all in the back room of the store. While Jeremy handled the incoming produce, which had to be taken care of right away, Echo moved palettes around with an old fashioned forklift to make room for more. By noon, she had gotten most of them inside, making a narrow pathway for walking through the room. Another worker signed for groceries from three more delivery trucks that arrived before noon. Echo had hoped to have time to daydream during this job, but maybe when things slowed down, if they slowed down, she would not have to work so hard.

She and Jeremy sat down at one of the loading docks and ate their lunches, which were delivered from a truck.

"I'm glad you decided to help out," Jeremy said. "We needed it, as you can see."

"I don't know how you got along without more help," said Echo. She dripped a little ketchup from her hotdog onto her jeans and wiped it off with a napkin. Jeremy watched her. She looked up and their eyes connected. "What's wrong?"

"Nothing." He turned away. He finished off his hot dog and wiped his mouth. He turned back to her. "I just wish you would stay working here at the store permanently."

"Thanks, but you know I want to stay with USSA."

"I know." Jeremy's watch chimed. "Well, back to work." They both stood up. Jeremy brushed the crumbs off his jeans. "Don't worry, once we catch up, the work will be easier. You might even get bored."

"I hope so," said Echo. They both laughed.

Echo just couldn't get the cave out of her mind. It seemed to be calling to her in her night dreams as well as her daydreams. So she decided to take off three days from work and fly to Spike. There, she rented an all-terrain vehicle called a Jeeper Creeper and drove to the cave.

As she slowly drove into the cave, she felt a sense of eeriness. Being by herself might have had something to do with it, but she sensed there was more.

Echo laid out her belongings—blankets and bedding—on the precipice where she and the captain had slept the last time they were there. Except this time, she brought lots of padding for her bed as well as a pillow. She also placed several heat globes around the cave that would activate once it got dark. She brought only raw food to eat, as she didn't feel like going to the trouble of cooking over the fire pit. What she really felt like doing was simply sitting and listening.

Once Echo had set up her things, the eerie feeling subsided, and she began to feel at peace with being in the cave by herself. But she felt like she was not really alone. When she closed her eyes, she felt that spirits from the past, present and future joined her. However, she did not see any spirits, only felt their presence, if that was what they indeed were.

After sitting for a time, Echo lay down on her back and covered herself with some heavy blankets. Again, she closed her eyes, but this time, she had a vision of events that took place when she and the others had last been in the cave. In this vision, she was more of an observer than an active participant.

In the replay of what had happened during the thunderstorm, Echo saw the same medicine woman she had seen in her dream. She was dressed in traditional American Indian garb with feathers attached to her hair. She held one large white feather in her hand and waved it in front of Echo's eyes. Echo saw a huge vortex descend from the ceiling of the cave, and she knew that was what had caused her and the others to enter an alternate universe. But why had she, the captain, and Lucy, been given powers? In answer to her thoughts, the medicine woman waved her feather over Echo, then the captain, then Lucy, giving Echo the power of intuition, the captain the power of healing, and Lucy the ability to speak English. Why were the men not given powers? Or were they? No answer came. Then the medicine woman disappeared.

Echo opened her eyes and sat up, fearing she had been transported to an alternate universe. That would not be good. Her heart pounded. She examined the cave wall, but the drawings were the same as before. She relaxed and knew she was all right. She sat and meditated until the hunger pangs in her stomach interrupted her. She didn't know why she'd been given the heightened power of intuition, but she wanted to develop it and use it only for the benefit of herself and others. She hoped she could learn to use it at will instead of only having it come over her suddenly without warning.

She got up and peeked outside the cave. The sun was just setting. She felt very peaceful. She sat and waited until the sun completely vanished from the horizon. Then she went back inside the cave. The heat globes had activated, but she was still cold. She wished the captain and the others were there to keep her company. She missed the bond she felt among them all and longed for their companionship.

Echo removed a sandwich from her backpack and ate it a little too quickly. Then she had an apple. She felt lonely and thought about driving back to Spike, but she knew it was better to stay in the cave all night and drive back in the morning. Perhaps she would have a dream that would reveal more of the mystery of the medicine woman to her. However, when morning came, Echo could remember nothing of her dreams the night before.

Chapter 26
Dana Faces Davis

She had wanted to meet with Jump Davis right away and get it over with, but Dana found she needed to build up her strength. She started out by doing martial arts exercises at home for a half-hour a day. After a week, she ventured out to the USSA gym. Wilson went with her, and they sparred for fifteen minutes at a time after warming up with stretching exercises. Dana would rest on the bench, then spar again until she was exhausted. Wilson would urge her to slow down, but she forced herself. She slept well at night, and finally, after three weeks, she noticed she only had to take one short nap a day.

"I'm ready to face Davis," she told Wilson one day. They were still in bed. The morning January sun shone weakly through their bedroom window. Wilson sat up and looked at her lying on her back, staring at the ceiling.

"Are you sure?"

She sighed and sat up. "Yes. I'm going to contact the others today. They are probably wondering what happened to me. Jump probably thinks I chickened out too."

Wilson got out of bed and began dressing. "I guess you know what you're doing."

She laughed. "I'm unsure of the outcome, but you know I'm going to give it a try." She stretched her arms and her back, bending over in a yoga pose. Then she got out of bed and went into the facility for a shower. The water refreshed her, and she felt completely awake after dressing.

Downstairs, Wilson had already started the coffee. It smelled wonderful.

Dana purposely arrived at the restaurant early, so she could be composed when Jump Davis arrived. She wore a black jumpsuit and a lightweight tan leather jacket. Her gold earrings dangled when she turned her head to the approaching server who took her drink order. Now that her implant was gone, she was able to drink alcohol, but she wanted to be alert, so she ordered a ginger ale. Once she had her drink, she sat quietly, contemplating their meeting. She didn't want to do anything to encourage his advances. She only wanted to discuss a truce. He might even deny having anything to do with the break-in at her house or having her followed into the mountains. But she knew those events could only be his doing. She had no other enemies, and no one was obsessed with her like he was.

Finally, Jump arrived. He stood there for a moment and studied her with genuine pleasure. He still had his blond ponytail but was clean-shaven and wore a tan suit with a white shirt open at the neck and no tie. She could smell his aftershave or cologne, which was pleasant and not too strong.

"Hello, Dana. Good to see you," he said as he slipped into the booth. The server immediately arrived and took his drink order, a beer on tap.

"Hello, Jump. Thank you for agreeing to meet me."

"My pleasure," he said. His eyes lit up and she felt like running away. To think she was fool enough to fall for this guy at one time.

The server brought large printed menus, a luxury with the shortage of paper. Dana ordered a BLT sandwich with chicken noodle soup. Jump ordered fish and chips with coleslaw.

"So, what's on your mind, Dana? You haven't contacted me since you got back from your trip to the asteroid belt."

She gave him a serious look. "Are you aware that the replacement implant you gave me exploded several weeks after you gave it to me?"

Jump looked shocked, but she knew it was an act. "Of course not. It must have been a defective unit. You know I wouldn't want any harm to come to you."

"Of course not," she said with just an edge of sarcasm.

Dana didn't bring up her other issues while they were eating. They talked about his business and her house, for the most part. She didn't talk about Wilson and he didn't ask.

The server appeared again and brought the bill, which was on a small electronic tablet. Dana immediately grabbed it. She didn't want to be indebted to Jump for anything.

"Another drink?" the server asked.

"Yes," said Dana.

"I'll have another draft beer," said Jump, seeming happy he could spend more time with her.

Once the drinks arrived, she got right to the point. "I had a break-in at my house several months ago by two masked people who were trying to abduct me. Do you know anything about that?"

"Oh, that's terrible. No, I never heard about it. It wasn't in the news or anything. Why would anyone want to kidnap you?"

"That's what I'm wondering. And then I went on a road trip, and someone blew up the vehicle we were using."

Jump put his hands to his face. "That's awful! Say, Dana, I know a good detective. Would you like her name?"

Dana sighed. "No thanks. I've got a force field around my house now." She wanted him to know.

The server returned and took Dana's currency. "Thank you and please come again," he said.

"Thanks for lunch. I was going to pay," said Jump.

Once she finished her ginger ale and saw that Jump's glass was empty, Dana stood up. "You're welcome."

Jump stood up too, and they exited the restaurant, emerging into the bright sunshine. The day was clear and almost smog-free, so neither of them wore their breathers.

"Can I see you again?" Jump asked.

Dana cleared her throat. "Um, well, you know, I'm with someone."

"Oh, that's right. Coop Wilson, I believe?"

"Yes."

Dana was about to turn away when two people came up behind her and took her by each arm. She turned to her right to see one of them was Dallas Jones. The other was a tall lanky man. His face was shrouded with his hat, and she couldn't turn to get a good look at it anyway. This was the plan. Dallas and Davis' man, Slug Spillman, were supposed to abduct her, so she was not surprised, but she acted as if she were and struggled to get away.

"What's going on? Let go of me." She managed to break free from both of them and could have run, but she waited a split second for them to latch onto her again. I hope Dallas' recorders are working, she thought. She dare not turn around, or she would give her plan away, but the van containing her crewmembers should be coming around the corner about now. If not, it would latch onto the tracker in her foot.

Dallas and Slug shoved her into the back seat of a black limousine. Then a mask was jammed against her nose and mouth, and everything went dark.

Dana woke up lying on a hard surface. Her head ached, and her mind was groggy. She tried to sit up, but a large hand pushed her back down. The room was dimly lit, but she could tell the hand did not belong to Davis.

"Just stay where you are, Captain," said the unfamiliar male voice. The man wore a black mask over his eyes. He might have been Slug Spillman, but she wasn't sure.

"Who are you? Where's Jump?"

"Never mind who I am. Mr. Davis will be here in a moment."

"May I have some water?"

"I don't think I'm supposed to let you out of my sight. Sorry, Captain."

"Please. I can't go anywhere." She lifted her cuffed left hand and moved her bound legs back and forth.

The man hesitated. He didn't seem too bright, which was good for her. "Well, I guess it would be okay. He opened the door a crack and ducked out.

Dana tried to break free of her restraints but it was no use. As her eyes began to focus and her head began to clear, she glanced around the room. In front of her was some kind of shrouded figure. A statue, perhaps? To the right of her was a plain desk and one chair.

It wasn't long before the masked man came back into the room with a glass of water. It was stupid of him not to have brought a straw. Dana wiggled her arms. "Do you mind? I can't drink lying down." She watched as he waved his left wrist over one of her cuffs and it released. "Thanks. How about the other one?"

"Better not," he said.

"That's okay. I can manage." She boosted herself up and he put the glass to her mouth. She took one sip then suddenly jammed it into his face. He made a muffled sound. Then she grabbed his wrist and waved it over the other cuff. It popped open. The man staggered to his feet, but Dana used her martial arts skills to elbow him in groin. This time, he made a louder cry of pain and doubled over. She quickly unbuckled the restrains around her ankles, freed herself, and made a dash for the door. It easily opened, but Jump Davis stood in her way.

"Well, well now, Dana. I see you've outsmarted Slug Spillman here. He's not too smart anyway, but he is loyal to me, unlike my other former employee. He thrust a bound and gagged Dallas Jones through the door and shoved her into a chair. She was wearing what looked like a bathrobe and her feet were bare. "I've burned her clothing, so your little plan of capturing me on camera didn't pan out so well."

Dana's heart sunk. At least she knew for sure that Dallas was on her side. But they were both in deep trouble now.

Chapter 27
Rescue

Tommy TwoTrees had closely tailed the black limousine in a small rental van until it reached the skyscraper where Davis Enterprises resided. Echo watched eagerly as Tommy drove the van into the parking garage underneath the building.

"There it is," said Mackovich as she pointed to the black limo parked in the corporate space provided for it. She, Echo, Wilson, Tommy, and Anderson piled out of the van once it was parked next to the limousine. They all had concealed U-guns and were ready to liberate the captain, but the occupants of the limousine were long gone.

"Hurry, this way," said Mackovich as she pointed to the elevator. After they stuffed themselves into the elevator, Tommy quickly sprayed the elevator's cameras with black paint, and Mackovich shouted out the number, forty-nine, where Davis Enterprises offices were. But when they arrived, the elevator doors would not open.

"Try the floor below," said Echo, desperate for a solution. But the doors would not open to that floor either. "Dallas was supposed to let us in." Echo was disappointed, thinking Dallas had sold them out. But her disappointment quickly turned to anger, and she pounded on the elevator doors and spouted a few curse words.

Wilson gently grabbed her arms. "Hey, calm down, Strand. I understand how you feel. We'll figure something out."

Echo took a few deep breaths and relaxed as much as possible. "You're right. Sorry."

Fortunately, Anderson had worn a tool belt and immediately produced a tire iron. "Take us down one floor," he said. They all had trackers, but it was hard to tell which floor Dana was on. Along with a hatchet, the group managed to pry the elevator doors open, but once they stepped out, a loud alarm rang.

"We're in this now, might as well forge ahead, gang," said Wilson.

Again, Tommy took his can of spray paint and coated all the cameras he could find. Then Echo took the lead, urgently wanting to find her captain. The rest followed her to an unmarked door. The tracker silently showed the proximity to the captain a couple of meters away. "She's in here," said Echo. "I can't get the door open."

"Of course you can't," said Mackovich. "Move over and I'll decrypt it."

This was one time Echo didn't mind Mackovich's pushiness and stepped aside. As Mackovich was running her decipherer, two security guards appeared in the corner of the lab. Evidently they'd had to take the freight elevator, but they wasted no time.

"Hey you, stop what you are doing," a slightly overweight man in his mid-fifties said. Echo and the others turned around raised their hands, hiding Mackovich, who was still trying to unlock the door. "Bennie, search them," the guard ordered his partner, a younger man who seemed a bit too nervous to Echo.

Echo's mind was racing. Her U-gun was in her jacket pocket. All she had to do was distract the young man, and the four of them could overtake both the guards.

"Don't try anything," Bennie told the group. "The police are on their way."

"Got it," Mackovich whispered.

Bennie took his eyes off Echo for only a second, and she kicked his gun out of his hand and pulled her U-gun from her pocket. The older guard came closer, but Wilson, Anderson, and Tommy quickly overtook him and grabbed his gun.

Mackovich had not yet opened the door. She didn't know if Davis was inside and armed. The rest of the group used plastic binders to tie the guards' hands, then shoved them into chairs. Echo had conveniently brought a few bandanas with her. She tossed them to Wilson, who gagged the men and bound their feet and hands to the chairs.

"Ready?" said Mackovich, who was holding the door's handle.

"Do it," said Wilson.

Mackovich pulled the door up. It was dark inside, but they heard a muffled sound. Echo moved toward the sound and saw that it was Dallas, tied to a chair and gagged with heavy-duty tape. Mackovich ripped off the tape while Echo cut the rope with her laser knife.

"Ouch!" said Dallas more loudly than she intended to.

"Where's Dana?" said Wilson. Dallas turned and pointed toward where the captain was lying on a table, her head hooked up to electrodes.

"She can't move. Jump gave her something to paralyze her. He's downloading her mind into that—thing over there."

Wilson and Echo looked at a replica of the captain standing in the corner. It was eerie. Its blue eyes were hollow as if it were a dead person or a wax museum piece.

"We've got to get her out of here," said Wilson anxiously.

"Jump is the only one with the antidote, unless—.

"Unless what?" said Echo.

"Unless he decides to kill her. You'd better get out of here," said Dallas. "Jump and Slug will be back any minute."

"We're not going anywhere without Dana," said Wilson.

"I don't know what'll happen to her if we just rip her apart from the machine," Dallas said.

Wilson frowned. "There's got to be a way."

Outside the room, Mackovich shouted to Wilson and Echo. "The police are on their way. I hear the sirens."

"Try and hold them off. Jam all the elevators."

"Okay."

"And get someone to intercept Davis and a guy named Slug."

"Got it," said Mackovich, sounding as confident as ever.

Echo wished she had Mackovich's confidence. She was extremely worried about the captain. She went over and stood next to the captain. She was awake and aware to all that was going on. She could move her eyes, but that was all. "We're going to get you out of this, Captain." She started looking for the power supply to the machine that was transferring the captain's mind into the robot. But she stopped and looked the captain in the eyes. The captain's eyes went back and forth as if telling her not to tamper with anything.

"You don't want me to unplug you, right?"

The captain's eyes moved up and down, for a yes.

"Okay, we'll just have to get Jump to give you the antidote and hold off the cops."

The captain's eyes seemed to relax.

"Everyone get out of here," ordered Wilson. "I'll take care of Davis and the Slug."

"You'll need some help," said Echo. "I'm staying."

"You are too stubborn at times, Strand. All right. We'll hide behind this replica of Dana."

The others rushed out of the room, and Wilson shut the door.

In a few minutes, Echo heard someone approach. Davis opened the door then slid it closed again. "Someone's been in here," he muttered. Clearly, he couldn't ask the captain. He glanced around the dimly lit room. "Dallas is gone." He sighed. "I'll get her later." He quickly checked his computer and the electrodes on the captain's head. "Almost done."

Wilson slipped out from behind the android and stuck Davis in the side with his U-gun. "Okay, Davis, give her the antidote."

Jump Davis was surprised, but he just smiled. "Coop Wilson, what an unpleasant surprise." He looked down at the U-gun. "Not much of a weapon, Wilson. Only three stun shots to it and if you put me out, you won't get the antidote."

"I'll find it somehow," said Wilson.

"Well now, I've got a man right outside the door with an assault rifle, fully laser loaded. You won't get far even if you do put me out."

Just then, Echo emerged from behind the android and shot three stuns into Jump Davis, one in his side, one in his lower back, and a third in his hip. He fell to the floor, Wilson catching his gentle fall.

Wilson looked shocked. "Strand, I didn't see that coming."

"Neither did he."

Wilson removed his comm unit from his sleeve pocket. "Mackovich, where are you? Uh-huh? Okay. Davis is down, but there may be a man outside the door. Okay. Wilson out."

Echo waited anxiously as Wilson finished the call. "So?"

"We wait here and hope Slug didn't hear this conversation. Mackovich and the others are going to try and take him out. They disabled all the elevators, but there's nothing they can do about the stairs. If the police come, they'll have a long climb, but they'll make it up here.

"Do you think we can find the antidote?" Echo asked Wilson.

"I surely hope so."

"Maybe the captain knows. We can ask her 'yes' and 'no' questions."

Just then, they heard a bumping sound against the door. Echo heard muffled vocal sounds, then a loud thump. Shortly after that, the door opened, and Mackovich stood there with Tommy TwoTrees and Anderson, looking proud of their work. The tall man was slumped to the floor, unconscious.

Behind them came four blue clad uniformed police officers, pistols in their hands. Echo sighed. "How are we going to explain our way out of this?"

"Just tell them the truth," said Wilson. "I'll take care of it."

Chapter 28
Recovery

Dana opened her eyes to a white ceiling. It took her a moment to orient herself and remember she had been paralyzed. She tried moving her arms and then her legs. They worked. She turned her head to the left and saw a table with a pitcher of water and a glass with a straw. She tried to sit up, but it was too much of an effort. She felt groggy but didn't have a headache.

"She's awake," a female voice said. The woman moved closer, and Dana noticed she was dressed in pink nurse's scrubs. "How are you feeling?"

"Not sure yet," said Dana. She tried sitting up again but failed. "I'm really tired."

The nurse gently pushed her back down, then raised the top of her bed so that Dana could see her surroundings. "Just take it easy."

It took a few moments for her mind to focus. She noticed there was an IV in her arm. "What's this?"

"Just saline and water. You were dehydrated."

"Where are my friends?"

The nurse didn't answer that question. "A detective is outside in the hallway. He'd like to ask you a few questions if you're up to it."

A pang of apprehension hit Dana's heart. "Yes, please, send him in."

A tall slim man in his mid-forties entered the room. His suit was tan and he wore a maroon tie with diagonal grey stripes. His hair was blond, almost white, and contrasted nicely with his medium brown skin and hazel eyes. He walked over to her bedside and introduced himself.

"I'm Detective James Overmeyer. I'd like to ask you a few questions regarding your ordeal."

"What can I do for you, detective?"

"We have questioned Jump Davis, and he claims your friends broke into his office and assaulted both him and his colleague."

Dana frowned. "Where *are* my friends?"

"They are being questioned at the police station."

Dana's heart pounded. "My friends were there to rescue me. I hope you aren't detaining them against their will."

"Mr. Davis claims you went with him willingly."

"He kidnapped me." Her memories of the recent events were coming back rapidly.

"One of your friends, Dallas Jones, told us that the alleged kidnapping was staged—that you were trying to catch Mr. Davis in the act of abducting you."

"Yes, and we did. Dallas was supposed to have recorded the event, but Davis destroyed her camera."

"I see. Well that's what Ms. Jones told us."

"Where is Jump Davis now?"

"He is in another room in this hospital, recovering from the stuns that were inflicted upon him by Ms. Echo Strand."

"Inflicted?" Dana was growing angrier. "He paralyzed me, hooked electrodes to my head, and transferred my memories into his android. Did you confiscate that?"

"No, that is Mr. Davis' property."

"And my mind is my property," said Dana.

"Captain, I just wanted to get your side of the story, and it corroborates with what your friends told us. However, there is no hard evidence that Mr. Davis took you to his office and performed the procedure against your will. Your friends will be released. You can press charges against Mr. Davis if you want, but he may be pressing charges against your friends as well. I will leave you to rest now."

Dana had a hard time calming herself but finally fell back to sleep. When she awoke later, Wilson was sitting next to her bed.

"Wilson." She reached her hand out to him. He took her hand, stood up, and leaned over her bed.

"How are you feeling?"

"Still tired."

"I'm glad you can move around. You had us all worried for a while.

"How did you get the antidote?"

The hospital did a blood analysis and came up with one. That took a while."

"How long have I been here?"

Wilson hesitated. "Almost two days."

"Two days!"

"So you and the others were detained for more than twenty-four hours."

"Yes, but there was no evidence to keep us."

"Is Jump still in the hospital?"

"That's the other thing. He's gone. He must have left when no one was paying attention. He wasn't officially released."

"What about that man of his?"

"He escaped."

"What a mess I've gotten you all into," said Dana. "I just wanted Davis off my back, and now he could get us into trouble."

Wilson sat down again. "Don't worry about it. We all wanted to help. It just backfired, that's all. Don't blame yourself. Davis is a psycho. He'll get caught eventually."

"Yeah, downloading my brain into his android. More than obsessed with me."

"For sure."

"So when do I get out of here?"

"I can go check."

"You'd think with my healing abilities, I would have been out of here by now."

"Maybe your abilities only apply to cuts and scratches. I'd like to know how far they go."

"Me too, but I sure wouldn't want word to get out. I'd have a long line of people at my doorstep."

"Be right back." Wilson left her room to find a health care worker.

Chapter 29
Reward

"Am I hearing you right? You want me to be XO on your crew?"

"Yes, unless you don't want the position."

"Uh, yes, I would be honored, but Captain, I really don't deserve it."

"Oh, I think you do. You've been on the team that Wilson is now captain of for seven years. And five of those years you were lieutenant commander. You also commanded seventeen shuttle trips to the moon and back. I think you are qualified."

"Captain, I haven't told you everything about my work for Jump Davis. And after you hear this, you may have a change of heart."

They were sitting in Captain Stewart's office at the USSA base. The captain was sitting behind her desk and Dallas was sitting in front of it. At first, when Captain Stewart called her in, she thought she was in big trouble. After all, she up and quit her job and also acted impulsively at times. She had seen a psychologist and gone to anger management classes before she took the job loading nuclear waste onto rockets. But she still held some resentment about not being promoted to XO on her own team.

"Sometimes our anger is useful," the captain continued. "If we can keep it in check.'"

"How so?"

"Well, in emergency situations our anger can give us the energy and motivation to creatively come up with solutions."

"I wasn't much help getting you out of the jam with Davis."

"But you were willing to jump right in and give it a try."

Dallas hung her head down for a moment, then she looked into Captain Stewart's intense blue eyes. "Yes, I sometimes jump right into situations before thinking."

"I'm sure you are working on that. But what I admire about you, Dallas, is that you have the courage to do so."

"Thank you, Captain. But I need to be honest with you."

"Yes?"

It was difficult for Dallas to get what she wanted to say out of her mouth, and she paused. But the captain waited. "I was one of the people who broke into your house. Slug Spillman was the other. Jump Davis offered us a quarter million each to kidnap you. He said he only wanted to see you for a day or two and then would let you go, but when I found out how psycho he was, I got out of it."

"I see," said Captain Stewart. "Well, I'm glad you told me the truth." The captain's look turned inquisitive. "How did you happen to get mixed up with him in the first place?"

Dallas took a deep breath and let out a sigh. "I had quit USSA and was out of a job. I applied several places but didn't even make it to the interview stage, but when I applied to Davis Enterprises, I was called in. I was responding to an opening in their research department, as I have a bachelor's degree in applied physics. But Jump said he wanted me to find you. I was almost out of money, so I agreed, especially since he gave me and Slug a three thousand dollar payment up front."

"So you were desperate."

"Yes, but there is no excuse for what I did. I could have collected unemployment, but that amount could hardly sustain my livelihood. Sometimes I act impulsively and take the consequences later. I'm surprised you were willing to trust me after you found out I dropped that tracker into your pocket."

Captain Stewart looked thoughtful. "I have been told I trust people too much, but I believe in giving a person a second chance, and you proved yourself by helping me set up that fake kidnapping."

"Yeah, but all the video is gone. And Davis knows he can't trust me now."

"Speaking of Jump Davis, do you have any idea where he is?"

"My guess is he left the planet."

"That's right. He has a uzerium mine on Mars. He slipped through the fingers of the police again."

"Captain, may I ask you something?"

"Of course." Her eyes bored into Dallas, but Dallas wasn't intimidated.

"You don't seem angry. If someone did to me what Jump did to you, I'd be fuming. I'd want revenge."

"Believe me, Dallas, I have those feelings, but I have to control them. They will just get me into trouble."

"Isn't it hard?"

"To control them? Yes, it certainly is. But I think Jump and I will meet again. Somehow, sometime, this issue will be resolved. At least that's what I believe." Her eyes softened.

"Well Captain, I can't thank you enough for your confidence in me."

Captain Stewart stood up. "You just show me what a fine officer you can be. We'll be taking off early Friday morning. The captain shook Dallas' hand. Her handshake was firm but so was Dallas'.

"Yes, Ma'am."

As Dallas walked back to her living quarters she still shared with Echo Strand, she wondered how Strand and the rest of the crew would respond to her instant status of second in command. The ship wouldn't be large like the *Midnight Mover* that the Stewart team had taken to Mars with passengers and huge tanks of liquid nitrogen. This ship was smaller and faster. It would only take them less than two weeks to get to Mars using their new hyper drive. They could only use the hyper drive in short bursts, a few seconds at a time, as using it for longer would burn out the engines and fry their inertial dampers. But the new technology made it possible to travel to and from Mars any time of the year rather than wait for the window when Mars was closest to Earth. Therefore, no one would have to go into status, so it was very likely that Dallas would be in command on the bridge for a third of the time, if shifts were taken every eight hours.

Dallas approached her quarters and opened the door. Strand was not home. She was probably still working at her mother's grocery store or cruising around in her new vehicle. But it was not like Strand to engage in unproductive recreational activities. She seemed so serious most of the time. Lately, she spent a lot of her spare time in meditation and her often far away look made her seem as though she were in touch with another world, especially since she had returned from her weekend visit to the mountains.

Chapter 30
Revealing

Echo was busy with her diagnostic on the AI that operated the small freighter, *Sure Thing*, which was loaded with frozen food, the majority of it meat. Its cargo also included computers and communications devices, packed in the cargo hold as tightly as possible.

She was in a sullen mood as she ran the routine diagnostics. She wasn't sure why she felt as she did. The last time she'd gone to Mars, she was quite excited. Perhaps she was sad that Wilson wasn't along for the flight. His ship was due to leave Earth for Mars in a week from now. She was mildly annoyed that Dallas Jones was assigned as XO to replace Wilson. After all, she had broken into the captain's house and actually tried to abduct her. How could the captain be so trusting? Didn't she ever get angry? She had been betrayed more than once—even by a former crewmember who had sabotaged a fuel cell in the captain's spaceplane in order to delay the delivery of weapons to the Resistance. At least that incident had cleared an opening for Echo to join Captain Stewart's crew permanently. Still, Echo liked Dallas and didn't feel any ill will toward her personally. She just felt irritated at the situation.

As she was pondering these thoughts, lost in her own world, Captain Stewart approached her from behind, startling her.

"How's it going, Strand?"

Echo sat up straight and looked the captain in the eye. "Almost done. I'm finding only a few minor glitches, which have already self-repaired."

"That's good. We'll have a crew meeting here on the station in room three zero two at sixteen hundred."

"When do we depart?" Echo asked solemnly.

"We're scheduled for zero six hundred tomorrow."

"Okay." Echo went back to focusing on her work.

"Something going on with you that I should know about, Strand?" The captain's voice held concern, but it was not harsh.

"No. I passed the physical. Why?" Echo was surprised at her own defensive tone.

"Well, the last time we went out, you were a bit more enthusiastic." Captain Stewart leaned against a stool next to Echo.

"Sorry, Captain. I'll try to cheer up." Her words were not sarcastic, but her heart felt heavy.

"There's a lot of fear out there, Echo. And I don't mean about the stars and hard vacuum. It's a way of looking at the world. There is also a lot of fear mongering, especially in the economy right now. That's why the government wants uzerium right away. There are more and more ships turning up at Mars with deliveries and going back to Earth with uzerium. You are a good and faithful crewmember. You do your job well, and I appreciate your loyalty."

"But?" Echo said even before totally processing what she had just heard. For some reason, anger momentarily stirred in her. She pushed it away.

"Can you tell me what's bothering you?"

"Sorry for my mood. You need your crew working as a team. I will do my best." Echo was silent for a moment.

The captain just waited while Echo finished her diagnostic. Then Echo turned to her. "I shouldn't be, but I'm a little bothered that you gave Dallas the XO position. How can you trust her?" Echo's words came out in controlled anger.

"I just do. And," she paused, "I trusted *your* judgment about her. But I'll tell you something. My intuition is also improving."

Echo didn't know what to say to that. She only thought that her accuracy with her job, her accountability, and her loyalty would be worth more than what Dallas had to offer. Then she sighed, as if realizing there was no basis for her jealousy. "I'm sorry. I don't know what's gotten into me, Captain. I certainly don't want to be XO."

She smiled. "Oh, so you admit to being human." The captain smiled.

Echo sighed. "Well *you* never seem to get angry. And look at all you've been through."

"Oh, I get angry, but I take a lot of it out in martial arts. And you don't see me all the time. But the point is, if something is bothering you, don't shut down. And you don't have to knock yourself out trying to be perfect. Just relax and be yourself."

"Okay, Captain." Echo leaned back in her chair.

"And, as for trusting people? I *have* to trust. Even though Dallas did some stupid things, she has the guts to own up to what she did. She is also decisive to a certain degree, which I want and need in a first officer. She's got an adequate amount of experience under her belt too."

"You're right. Dallas is a good choice for XO."

Captain Stewart put a firm hand on Echo's shoulder. Then she stood up and headed for the door. "See you at the meeting, Strand."

Echo felt spacy, pondering the conversation. She also felt lighter. Not totally, but as if a few weights had been removed from her shoulders. There was still a gnawing in there—in her body. It wanted out. She couldn't identify the source. Echo checked her watch, then she got into a float tube, one of many in Atlantis Station, and checked herself into the USSA gym.

Chapter 31
Android Blues

Jump Davis walked through the door of his home in the domed community on Mars after a long day in his office. Most of his time was spent in his luxurious office on the fifth floor of the office complex, but he liked to oversee the uzerium mines himself, so he would tour the mining areas from time to time. He owned two mines, both purchased from TransCom. Mining took longer these days, since each load had to be tested for impurities. A couple years ago, bacteria had been found in one of the mines that Jump now owned. But since that time, the newly found ore had little or no bacteria. Jump bought both mines easily for a good bargain.

Jump removed his jacket and hung it over a chair. "Hi, Dana, I'm home."

The android he had built activated by hearing his voice. It walked into his common room more slowly than the real Dana would have, but its looks were strikingly similar. So was its voice.

"Hello, Jump. How was your day?"

"Long and tiresome." He slumped into a chair. "Would you please massage my shoulders?"

"Of course, dear. Sit up and relax."

The massage movements of its fingers and hands on his shoulders and neck were mechanical but still felt good. He could tell it to slow down or speed up or move its hands to a different spot or even apply more or less pressure. But it didn't feel like a real person doing the work, and of course, it wasn't. A good masseuse would have instinctually known how and where the tight muscles were.

"That's enough for now."

The Dana android stopped abruptly. "What would you like now, Jump?" it said softly.

Jump stood up and looked the android in the eye. Its eyes had been made well. He had ordered them from a special vendor, an expensive one, but worth the money. The eyes had the intense blue stare that the real Dana had at times. Jump took its hand and led it to the kitchen. "You can fix my dinner."

"What would you like?"

"The rice, beef, and vegetable packet will do."

"Certainly." The android dropped his hand, went to the kitchen, took the food packet out of the freezer and placed it into the convection oven. While the meal was cooking, the android set a place for him at the table.

He watched its movements. They were only slightly robotic. He would have to tweak it so that it moved more slowly and gracefully.

When his dinner was served, the android sat across the table from him and watched him eat. The android had no internal organs, only machine parts and circuitry. He had programmed it to say and ask of him certain things, but he hadn't had time to install an artificial intelligence in it. Perhaps not having an AI was a safer way to go anyway. If it began to think for itself, it could take the memories the real Dana had and turn against him, maybe even override the safety protocols. It had happened before to other people's androids. Another drawback was that although the android could show a semblance of affection by putting its arms around him and speaking sweetly to him, he strongly sensed it wasn't real and it had no heart, no soul. After a couple of weeks of living with the android, Jump longed again for the real Dana. He would rather have the real Dana even if it meant she would yell at him and show no affection. The real Dana had fight, had spirit, and most importantly, could make love to him. Not that she would at this point.

The longing was worse at night. It tore him up inside. And to think he seriously wanted her dead a few times. Would the longing go away if she were dead? He didn't know. Keeping her against her will wouldn't work either—wouldn't give him the satisfaction he really wanted. If he could just get over her. He was angry. The android was not working out for him.

The next morning when Jump consulted his computer, he found that a USSA freighter that Dana was captaining was due to arrive in thirty-seven hours. It was after a load of uzerium. Unfortunately, it was not picking up the ore from his company. He wouldn't have an excuse to see Dana. He had to admit to himself that he could never have her.

Jump had caught a private spaceplane to Vegas Space Station immediately following the police raid of his research lab in Los Angeles, taking Slug Spillman and his android with him. Slug had barely escaped the police by using an escape chute in the building, dragging along Jump's shrouded android, not an easy task. Slug stayed hidden until Jump escaped from the hospital and met up with him. Then they hopped a skycab to a small spaceport in Nevada. Jump chose to go to Vegas Station because Atlantis Station had a strong USSA presence. From Vegas Station, they hired an illegally registered ship to take them to Mars. The price he had to pay for all this transportation was worth escaping from the police in Los Angeles.

He wouldn't admit he was ashamed of having the Dana android. Other people bought android companions, many fashioned after celebrities or loved ones who'd passed on. But some part of Jump *did* feel ashamed. When those feelings and thoughts occasionally touched his consciousness, he became angry and tried to shut them out.

Chapter 32
Landing

"Captain, I don't think you should leave the station," Strand said, once the supplies had been unloaded from *Sure Thing*. This time, Mars workers unloaded the supplies and loaded them onto the landers, while *Sure Thing's* crew waited. On Dana's last trip here, her crew had to unload their own cargo.

The workers were dressed in rust red government jumpsuits with black stripes down the arms and legs. They wore small caps with Mars government insignias on the front.

Each container was scanned for contents and checked by a computerized manifest, while the crew waited.

"This is ridiculous," Mackovich said. We could be on the planet, going about our business instead of standing around here on this puny space station."

That comment got her a look of disapproval from one of the government workers, but he only went on checking the containers.

"Easy does it, Mack," said Dana. "Things have changed since we were last here."

"Sure have." She folded her arms and stood impatiently.

"Captain, I have a bad feeling about you going down to the surface," Strand quietly told her.

"Strand, I can take care of myself."

"I know."

But Dana was curious. "Can you be more specific?"

"Not sure, but it may have something to do with Jump Davis."

Dana and the others stood by as the workers loaded the last of the cargo into the landers. "There is plenty of security in the dome. Besides, if he is here, he's probably at his mining facility. And, our pickup is from a different company."

"I know that," said Strand. "I just think it would be safer for you to stay here on the station. I'm sure there are plenty of accommodations for visitors."

"That may be, but I'm not going to tiptoe around my life just because of Jump Davis. He's got his android of me. That ought to satisfy him for a while."

One of the workers must have overheard their conversation and spoke up. "The captain has to sign for the cargo in person, so she *has* to go down."

"There, you see, Strand? The decision has already been made."

"Just be careful."

Dana smiled. "I appreciate your loyalty. You don't need to follow me around as a body guard though."

"And if I prefer to?"

"If you *prefer* to, I won't stop you."

The orbiting space station did have plenty of accommodations, entertainment, shops, and restaurants, because Mars government workers lived there. The main dome on the planet was more spacious with more shops. Dana really missed Wilson. He was on his way here on his own ship and wouldn't arrive for another week. Shopping would keep Dana busy. She wanted to buy some souvenirs and unique paper and pencils for her daughter. The composite paper and pencil material was made from Mars' regolith combined with other materials.

"Okay, *Sure Thing* crew, you may board Lander Number Six."

"It's about time," said Mackovich, not too loudly as to irritate her captain, but Dana gave her the eye anyway. Secretly, Mackovich amused Dana with her straightforward, rough exterior.

One by one, they filed into the small craft, Dana last, and strapped themselves in. Other passengers already sat paratrooper style in the windowless lander. A worker checked their harnesses, then gave the "good to go" signal to the launch person.

Once the lander detached from the docking clamps, the passengers became momentarily weightless. This was always a thrill to Dana. And then the rockets boosted them toward the planet, and Dana felt the heat of the atmospheric entry, but not as much as she had the last time she was here. They must have improved the shielding, she thought. And it wasn't as bumpy of a ride as she'd had before either. Strand was sitting beside her and surprised Dana by taking her hand. Good, Dana thought. She's letting herself be vulnerable. Dana squeezed Strand's hand and held it until they landed, neither of them looking at each other. Once on the surface, their seatbelts unclasped, and they were ordered to disembark by an automated voice.

Once inside the dome, Dana told Strand she was going to sign for the shipment and then do some shopping. To go to the company where the uzerium was coming from, Dana would have to take the underground maglev train. Strand insisted on going with her. None of the other crewmembers were concerned, as Mars security people were literally everywhere.

After they had acquired some Mars currency, Strand followed Dana through the concourse that would take them to the underground train depot. Their wristcodes worked for fare as they had the last time they were there. But unlike the last time she was there, every passenger had to go through a security check and surrender any weapons or anything that could be used as weapons. Like the old airline days, Dana thought. She had brought a U-gun as had Strand. The U-gun stunners were standard issue for spaceship crew as well as security guards. Dana reluctantly gave up her weapon and thought at least she was well versed in martial arts. They couldn't take away her arms and legs. Lately, Strand had been learning some martial arts as well, but she was only a beginner.

Entering the train, she went instantly from one gravity to one-third gravity. It was quite a sensation. Handlebars were everywhere. Dana grabbed the first one she saw and righted herself immediately after having her feet come out from under her as she entered. After six stops, Dana and Strand arrived at their destination, where Dana was to sign for the uzerium shipment. A government representative escorted them to the office, which was on the third level of a five-story complex, the same building in which Jump Davis had his office the last time she was here. Strand followed closely behind her. Two guards followed behind them. Obviously, government personnel and dealings in uzerium were more plentiful than before. The Mars government now owned half the mines, she was told. Our U.S. president would approve of this, she thought.

The office was all plastiglassed in and had a three hundred and sixty-degree view of its surroundings. On one side, an excellent view of one of the mines could be seen. The company representative ushered Dana and Strand to a couple of nicely made padded chairs, while he dialed up his computer wallscreen, which showed as transparent because of the plastiglass walls. He then showed a live feed of her order being loaded onto her ship.

"One hundred fifty-seven metric tons of unprocessed ore. Please sign here." He handed her an electronic pad.

"I'd like to wait until it's all loaded, if you don't mind," Dana told him. It occurred to her that the supposed live feed could be a recording, but she had left Tommy TwoTrees on the station to oversee the loading procedure.

The man stood back, still holding the pad. "Of course."

Dana glanced at Strand. Her eyes were sharp like a hawk's. They darted from the representative, to the door, ever watchful for danger. Dana wondered if Strand sensed something that was about to happen, but she dismissed the worry. There was nothing she could do right now but wait for the shipment to be loaded and get out of there. She looked back over at Strand. The young woman was still—no wringing hands, no jumpy legs. But she was totally present the entire time as if she were waiting for something to happen. Good discipline on her part, Dana mentally noted.

Finally, the shipment was loaded and the cargo doors locked. Tommy gave her the okay signal through the camera. "All right, Mr.?"

"McManus. Howard McManus."

"Mr. McManus," she acknowledged and signed for the cargo."

"Right this way," he said.

Outside the office, a different government representative escorted Dana and Strand to the elevator, down to the underground tunnel. A second government representative was waiting outside the elevator. All of a sudden, Dana felt a U-gun pushed into her back. She could tell what it was by its size and vibration. She glanced at Strand, who also had a U-gun pushed into her back.

"Keep your head pointed straight ahead and nothing will happen," the man whispered to Dana. His voice sounded vaguely familiar. He was a few centimeters taller than she was, and she thought she could take him on if it weren't for Strand's captor, a woman a little taller than Strand.

The four of them walked silently to a parking garage. The man remotely unveiled a car, while the woman made sure Dana and Strand stood still. Then the captors put Dana in the front seat with the driver, the man, while Strand and the woman got into the back seat.

After several turns, it didn't take long for Dana to recognize the route the car was taking. They were on their way to the domed community where Jump Davis had his house.

Chapter 33
Danger

Echo and the captain were quickly ushered into the house and greeted by Jump Davis. The fake government representatives gave Jump a nod and left.

"Well, Dana, here we are again. And you brought your faithful sidekick," he sneered.

Echo frowned, but said nothing. She wanted to kick him in the face, but now was not the time. He had a gun pointed at both of them, but the captain stayed calm. But what was he going to do with them?

"Have a seat, ladies," Jump said. He pointed to his couch, which faced a wallscreen that interchanged Earth nature scenes every few seconds.

"What do you want, Jump?" the captain asked.

"I want you. My android is not working out. She needs more from you."

"More what? You can take my memories, but you can't transfer my feelings into that thing."

"Oh, I don't know about that. That's what I'm going to find out. It'll be my great experiment."

"You're sick, you know that?"

Echo agreed, but she said nothing. She didn't want to make matters worse.

"Why don't you let Strand go? She has nothing to do with this."

Jump still had the gun pointed at both of them. "I think I'll keep her here. She could be a liability if I let her go."

"And what will you do with us once you are done?"

Jump smiled cynically. "I haven't figured that out yet."

Echo was nervous and wished she had the captain's composure. He was probably going to kill them or do away with them somehow. He couldn't have them leaving and telling the authorities he had kidnapped them. All the time she was plotting how to kick the gun out of his hand. Then she and the captain could overcome him, but she didn't move in time. Jump Davis called in his android.

Although Echo had seen the android before, this was the first time she had seen it in motion, and she was shocked at the likeness it had to her captain.

"Please bind their hands, Dana."

The android obeyed. When it spoke, it was the captain's voice, but stilted a bit. Echo wanted to activate the camera on her wristcomm, but Jump would notice. Besides that, she would have to pull up her sleeve to do it.

"Don't try anything, ladies. My android has the strength of ten people."

Echo didn't believe him. She had read up on lifelike androids, and nothing in the literature had suggested they had superhuman strength. Echo and the captain said nothing, just held out their hands. The binders were made of a strong plastic and hurt Echo's wrists. The android placed binders on her ankles as well, but not on the captain's.

"Now, Dana, you come with me.

The captain stood up while the android and Davis ushered her into another room. Echo's mind raced. She had not been tied to the couch or a chair, so she would be able to stand up and jump or scoot around. But what could she do? Whatever she did, it would have to be done quietly and quickly.

Echo became calm. Some part of her knew they weren't going to die. No, this was not their time. Maybe the reality of the situation she and the captain were in would hit her later. But now, she had to figure out a way to free herself. Her eyes roamed around the room until they fell on an object that lay on Jump's spacious desk. She wasn't sure, but it looked like a laser cutter, with a small handheld sized tubular shape. Her hands were bound in front, so if she could get a hold of the cutter, she could at least free her ankles.

She stood up slowly. She shuffled forward, and the binders on her ankles tightened. Then she knew that the binders tightened when resistance was applied. Carefully, she held her wrists together so the binders wouldn't tighten. She shuffled forward again and made a half turn toward the desk, all the while, trying to be as quiet as possible. However, her heart was pounding so hard, it was difficult to believe it couldn't be heard in the next room where Jump had taken the captain. So much for feeling calm.

Once Echo reached the desk, she bent over and stretched her arms out to reach the object. When she did this, her wrist binders tightened to the point of causing pain. She suppressed the urge to yell. She took a deep breath to calm herself and picked up the object. It was small and light weight, which was to her advantage, but when she straightened out her body, she lost her balance and fell backward onto the desk chair, then slipped to the floor. The laser cutter fell from her hands and clattered to the floor with her. She scrambled to hide under the desk, but she knew that action was futile. Jump Davis opened the door where he had the captain, and stormed into the common room.

"Strand, what is going on?"

Echo didn't answer. It didn't take long for Jump to find her. He pulled her to her feet.

"What are you doing to the captain?" she boldly demanded.

"That's none of your concern. Now, if I can't trust you to sit still and wait, I'll have to tie you to a chair—an unmovable chair." His eyes bored into hers, but Echo kept her eyes on his, not letting on that he scared her.

"I need to use the facility." She really didn't need to use the facility, but doing so would buy her some time to think and he would have to free her wrists and ankles if only temporarily.

Jump hesitated as if he didn't believe her, but he really couldn't argue. He cut her bindings and ushered her into the facility, shutting the door. Now she was alone. She searched the small room for an escape door or window, but could find none. There was nothing on the ceiling above the shower, only a small fan, and nothing under the bath mat. Then she got an idea.

"You're taking too long, Strand. I don't want to embarrass you by coming in to get you."

"Be right out." Echo turned on the sink water to make it sound like she was washing her hands. While the water was running, she stepped into the shower and waited for Jump's patience to expire.

"Hey, turn off the water!" he yelled. When Echo didn't answer, Jump opened the door and stepped into the room. While he was turning off the water, Echo swung from the shower rod and kicked him full force in the head. He was knocked to the floor but not unconscious. While he stirred, Echo ran into the room where the captain was lying on a table with electrodes pasted to her head, ready to transfer her brain waves into the Dana android. Echo activated her wristcomm's camera and began recording.

"We don't have much time, Captain." Echo started pulling electrodes from the captain's head and freed her from the table straps.

Echo took another look at the android, which was motionless and stared straight ahead. It gave her an eerie feeling. The captain quickly got up from the table, took Echo's hand, and led her out of the room. Unfortunately, Jump Davis was waiting for them with an old fashioned pistol in his hand. It looked like the kind of gun police used in old movies Echo had seen.

"That was a stupid move you made, Strand."

"Leave her out of this," said the captain.

"I'm sorry, I can't. I'm afraid I'm going to have to dispose of you, Strand."

The captain stepped in front of Echo. "You don't need to kill her, Jump. It's me you want. Let her go, and you won't become a murderer. Believe me, it's the right thing to do."

"Step away, Dana. I'm not past killing you either. I'll figure out a way to program emotions into my android without your help."

"You don't need to kill anyone. Besides, I don't have that implant in my head anymore. I know you wanted that. It dissolved into my system."

Just then, Jump's eyes refocused on something beyond the two women. Echo turned her head. It was the Dana android. Jump must have remotely activated it, or it could have initiated its own activation if it had enough of the captain's mind integrated into it. Its eyes were glazed, and it looked as if it were angry. With Jump holding the pistol on them from the front, and the android approaching them from the rear, Echo saw no escape.

The android approached the captain, grasped her, and kicked Echo to the floor. "You must die," it told the captain. "Two of us cannot exist." Then the android swiftly stepped forward and grabbed the pistol from an unsuspecting Jump Davis, and then shot at the captain. But she dodged the bullet and positioned herself in front of Jump. Echo watched helplessly as she waited for an opportunity to attack the android.

"Stay put, Strand," said the captain.

But Echo couldn't. She hadn't had much martial arts training, but she was good with her feet. As she was about to kick the pistol out of the android's hand, a shot was fired. Echo automatically crouched and covered her head. She smelled the sulfuric odor of gunpowder and dared to look up. Jump Davis was sprawled backward against his desk with a bullet hole in his forehead. The captain was grappling with the android, and the pistol was on the floor, a few centimeters away from Echo.

"I could use your help now, Strand," the captain grunted as she struggled with the android.

Echo grabbed the pistol and tried to push it into the android's neck, but the android and the captain were moving and turning too fast, and she feared she would hurt the captain.

Several times the captain would get the android into a position for Echo to shoot, but by the time Echo aimed, the android would switch positions with the captain.

"Help me push it into the corner," the captain said.

Echo stuffed the pistol into her jumpsuit pocket, and with all the strength she could muster, helped the captain push the android into a corner near the facility. Then came the arduous task of turning it around. Echo was pretty sure it had to be shot in the back of the neck at the base of the head to disable it. She had studied artificial intelligences and robots during her training at USSA.

The android fought back nobly, pushing and slugging and kicking each of the women in various places. But its efforts weren't enough. Finally, Echo and the captain pinned it to the floor and sat on it. The captain held its head.

"Okay, Strand, take your shot."

Echo struggled to pull the pistol from her pocket, almost not getting it out, as it temporarily got hung up inside her jumpsuit's thigh pocket while she was sitting on the android's body. Once the pistol was securely in her hand, Echo pushed it into the android's artificial skin and pulled the trigger. Immediately, the android became motionless, and slumped to the floor. The struggle was over.

Echo and the captain slowly got to their feet. They stood there for a moment, staring at the robot that resembled the captain.

"You okay?" the captain asked. Echo hadn't had time to think about having been battered and bruised.

"Yeah, I think so. How about you?"

"I'm okay," said the captain.

Echo walked over to where Jump Davis lay sprawled across his desk. "Why did it shoot him?"

"It was aiming for me. I ducked, and the bullet hit Jump."

"Whew, a close one."

"It's too bad he had to die."

"He was a fanatic."

The captain put her hand on her forehead. "Yes, but he wasn't always that way. Such a tragedy."

"He would have kept pursuing you as long as he was alive."

The captain sighed. "I suppose so. We'd better contact the authorities."

Before the captain could comm the police, Echo heard a knock on the door. She opened it. There stood the two fake government officials who had escorted them to Jump Davis' house in the first place.

Chapter 34
Truth Revealed

Dallas had gotten ugly stares when she first returned to USSA to apply for a job after having worked for Jump Davis. Now, as she approached the USSA operations office in the main Mars dome, she expected some people to be unfriendly as well. Word had gotten around that she'd lost her temper and made a scene when she wasn't promoted to captain on her ship, *Outbound*, and that Cooper Wilson had been named instead. So what? thought Dallas. I'm going in.

Standing at a semi-circular console were three young officers studying live shots of a ship leaving Mars Space Station, a cargo shuttle approaching the station, and a lander exiting the station. Another view screen showed shots of Mars' oddball shaped moons, Deimos and Phobos. The operator of that screen was zooming in and out of their views. So far, no uzerium or anything valuable had been found on those moons. To her right, uniformed ensigns studied transparent computer screens. Dallas couldn't quite see what was on them, but she guessed they were studying surveillance of various areas of the planet for clues of water or uzerium, both valuable resources. The curved wall to the left of the console displayed a large paper map of Mars as seen from the space station. A nice touch, Dallas thought.

Several heads turned as she entered the office. Their owners gave her a non-emotional stare, then turned back to their work. Friendly bunch, Dallas thought. She stepped over to the console.

"How's it going?" she asked a young lieutenant.

"Fine," said the woman, not further engaging Dallas in conversation.

"Good." Dallas stepped back. "I guess everyone is busy here, so I'll leave you to your work."

No one answered. So they *were* being snobs. She had expected that. It didn't bother her much. Just then, her left jacket sleeve lit up. She shoved up her sleeve to read the message on her wristcomm. It was from Captain Stewart. "Round up the others and come to the police station now."

Dallas exited the operations office and alerted the other members of her crew by forwarding the captain's message simultaneously to Strand, Anderson, Mackovich, Tommy TwoTrees, and Doc Sereno. The police station was on the other side of the two-kilometer wide dome, so she hopped on the pedestrian conveyor belt that circled the perimeter of the dome. The thing only went at one speed—slow—but it was faster than walking. While she was holding the rail, she answered the captain's message. "What's going on?" But there was no reply.

When she reached the police station, she was escorted into the interrogation room. She was told that Strand was in a separate room.

"What's going on?" she asked the sergeant.

"A man was killed, and your crewmates were in his house at the time."

Dallas' heart thumped and she felt her throat tighten. "Who?"

"Jump Davis. Did you know him?"

"Uh, yes, not well."

"Come this way, please."

The captain looked relieved to see Dallas as she walked into the room and sat next to her. "Jump Davis is dead?"

"That's right. Evidently, the police are questioning my story, even though Strand told the same story to them in a separate room."

"Well, what happened?"

Captain Stewart told Dallas what happened and how she and Strand had been taken against their will to Jump's house.

"So, the android killed him?"

"Yes, but it looks so much like me, the police are having a hard time believing me."

"They have video?"

"Strand activated her wristcomm after disabling Jump. They also have video of the man and woman who abducted us. That video was from the maglev. They want you or any of my crew to see if they can identify them."

"Sure, Captain."

By this time, the other crewmembers were arriving. Strand was also brought into the room. Three officers and all of Stewart's crew examined the video from Jump's home. Indeed, it looked as if Stewart aimed the gun at Jump Davis, with Stewart also ducking when the bullet hit Davis. In other words, the video didn't reveal which one of the Dana Stewart's was the android and which was the real person.

"If I were the one holding the gun at Davis," Stewart argued, "why would the android duck and let me shoot him? And why would I be pointing the gun at the android in the first place?"

"Because you didn't want it to survive," said one of the police officers. "Your partner killed the android, and you helped her."

"Yes, because it was after us. It was programmed to kill me. You heard it on the recording. It said, "You must die. Two of us cannot exist."

"That could have been you," said another police officer.

Stewart sighed. "Analyze the voice. That is a computerized voice."

"We're looking at that now," said the same officer.

Then they switched to the video from the maglev. "Do any of you recognize these people? They are impersonating government representatives."

"Please zoom in on that one," said Dallas. She studied the face. She was sure it was Slug Spillman. If she turned him in, he would surely expose her dealings with him as an accomplice to Jump Davis' scheme to capture Stewart. Captain Stewart had not reported her to USSA, so her record was clean as far as the agency was concerned. Being exposed would put a black mark on her record and might permanently ground her.

"Someone you recognize, Ms. Jones?"

Dallas hesitated only for a moment. "Yes. That's Slug Spillman. He's had some shady dealings with Jump Davis."

"And you know this how?"

"I'll save you some time. I used to be his partner."

Chapter 35
Homeward Bound

Dana woke to the chime of the monitor in her quarters. Still fuzzy headed, she commanded it on. It was Strand at her door with her supper. She sat up and ran her fingers through her hair. Her mind briefly went back to when the two police officers had brought in the slumped over android of herself. To think someone was so consumed with her that he would build an artificial life form as a substitute for the real her. Again, she felt more pity for Jump Davis than anger. In fact, the anger seemed to be gone. She and her crew had only been detained a day longer than their scheduled visit to Mars, but she was glad Strand had recorded the incident with her wristcomm. But it was Dallas' confession to having worked for Jump Davis that had completely cleared her and Strand of any foul play.

"Come on in, Strand." Her door swished open, and Strand entered with a tray of food complete with a container of hot coffee. "Set it down there," she said, pointing to a small table next to her bed. Strand obeyed then started to leave, but Dana stopped her. "Wait. Have a seat." Surprised, Strand sat down and gave Dana a curious look. It was the third day Dana had stayed in her quarters on their voyage home from Mars.

"How is Dallas doing?"

Strand shrugged. "Okay, I guess. She seems to be a natural commander. There's not a whole lot to do except monitor our inertial dampers and make sure the shield generator is on the high end of the percentage scale."

"Good. And everyone else is okay with her command?"

"They seem to be. They wonder how you're doing, though."

"Well, I guess I've been in my quarters long enough."

"I'm sure the crew would be okay with you staying here as long as you need to."

Dana uncovered her entrée. The welcoming aroma of pasta with marinara sauce caught her nose, and her stomach growled with hunger. She picked up her fork and dug in. "Umm. Very good. Have you eaten yet, Strand?"

"Yes, I have, Captain. We all had what you're having."

After a second bite, Dana wiped her mouth with the cloth napkin provided with her dinner. "Strand, tell everyone I'll be back on the bridge within the hour. I've rested enough."

After Strand left, Dana finished her meal, jumped into the shower, and put on a fresh jumpsuit. Her reflection in the mirror showed a slightly pale and thinner face than she was used to seeing. The ordeal with Jump Davis and the android as well as the grilling at the police station had taken a toll on her. And although she had acquired the ability to heal cuts and wounds with her hands, her own energy level needed restoration. The three-day rest in her quarters had helped. She could probably use more, but she was getting restless. However, she knew she would need her full strength in order to come across with a commanding presence. She could do it this "evening." She didn't know about tomorrow.

At first, no one noticed her entrance. Dallas was sitting in the captain's chair, Tommy TwoTrees was at the navigator station studying star maps, and Strand sat partially hidden from her view hunched over a small computer screen. Dana approached Dallas from behind and gently put her hand on the back of the chair, trying not to startle her. Dallas was startled though and jumped up from the chair. "Captain on the bridge," she announced. Tommy and Strand looked up and gave a nod, but didn't get to their feet.

Dana smiled. "As you were. No need to be so formal." Dallas slid into the chair to the left of the captain's seat, and Dana took her chair.

"Feeling better, Captain?" Dallas asked.

"Much. So how is our ship holding up?"

"So far, okay. Our day's delay didn't take us too far off our path. We have plenty of power reserves."

"Good to hear. Thanks for taking the helm for me."

"No problem."

Dana stood up and walked over to the navigation station. Tommy stood inside a hologram that showed the stars streaking by in real time. "May I?" Dana asked.

Without a word, Tommy stepped out and Dana stepped into the center of the holo.

"Darken it, will you, Tommy?"

Tommy did as he was told. Dana could still see the bridge of the ship, but she felt as if she were really out in the stars.

"This is fantastic. Now I know why you like your job."

Tommy wasn't much for words and answered with a simple nod.

Dana spent another minute or two inside the holo before stepping out again. "It makes me a little dizzy." Of course, she'd been in the holo several times before, but every time, it seemed like a new experience.

"You get used to it," Tommy said, his soft voice barely audible.

Dana then walked over to Strand's station at the AI. "How's it going?"

Strand was slow to look up. But when she did, her face was pale, almost ghostlike.

Dana's heart pounded and her muscles tensed. "What is it?"

"I don't know, Captain," she said quietly. "I have a strong sense of danger."

"What kind of danger?" Dana felt anxiety hit her with a jolt. Ever since she, Strand, and the others had come back from the alternate universe, Strand had been correct with her premonitions. The only problem was, she couldn't give details right away. Strand was undoubtedly experiencing her own anxiety, though she hid it well.

"I don't know. Maybe something will come to me."

"Take a deep breath, Echo." Dana rarely used the young woman's first name, but it just popped out of her mouth. Strand did as she was told. In fact, they both sat and breathed slowly and deeply for a moment. Then a light came to Strand's eyes as if she had received more information.

Strand looked into Dana's eyes. "We have to reserve power."

"Okay, why?" Dana said slowly.

"We'll need it for the deflector shields."

"Because?"

Strand shook her head as if trying to free her mind of cobwebs. "I don't know. I can't see that far ahead."

Dana stood up and began to pace, and then she sat down again, not wanting to alert the other bridge crew of her nervousness. "Well, if we need our shields powered more than they are now, it could mean we'll be encountering something out there that could damage our hull."

"But what could be strong enough to penetrate three layers of self-healing hulls?"

"I don't know, unless we run into a meteor shower or some very huge piece of space junk."

"I think we'll be okay if we reserve our power for the rest of the trip," Strand offered, some color returning to her face.

"Okay, I'll tell the rest of the crew Mackovich and Anderson aren't going to like it though. They've been using a lot of interactive game simulations."

"We could turn off the gravity in the cargo holds and crew quarters when people are sleeping."

"We'll just have to tie down the cargo really good. We can't have bags of uzerium knocking around in there."

"What will you tell the others?"

Dana sighed. "I'll tell them the truth."

"That I have a hunch?"

"I don't have to say it's *your* hunch."

"Say what you need to say, Captain."

Dana tapped Strand on the shoulder. "Better to be safe. I trust your instincts, Strand."

"Do the others know about our little journey to the alternate universe?"

"No, only Wilson. In fact, his ship should reach Mars in about ten days." Dana's eyes opened wide. "Is he in any danger?"

Strand answered immediately. "I don't sense any."

Dana commed the rest of the crew to the bridge. It took several minutes for the doctor to arrive, and a few more minutes for Mackovich and Anderson to slowly drag themselves up through the lower hatch. Dana could hear their slow steps clanking up the metal stairway, as if reluctant to leave whatever activities they'd been engaged in.

"Okay, everyone. We have to reserve power for the rest of the trip," Dana said when they were all gathered together.

Anderson frowned. "How come? We have plenty of power. Our engines are working at peak efficiency."

"Yeah, what are we supposed to do if we can't play our games?" said Mackovich, always the complainer, but that was just her style. She respected Dana and Dana knew it.

Dana held up both hands. "Calm down, you guys. Now, for the first question—why?" She looked out at the expectant faces of her crew. "We may need to use our deflector shields at full capacity."

"What's going on?" Dallas turned to her and asked.

"It's a hunch, and I'm going with it," Dana said without hesitation.

At that, Strand spoke up. "I'm the one with the hunch. Captain Stewart is just following my advice."

Dana admired the young woman for exposing her truth. "Let's just leave it at that, shall we?" Dana said. It was a rhetorical question, and she continued. "As to what you're to do," she beamed her steel blue eyes into Mackovich's, "you can start by tying down all the cargo. We're going to be turning off the gravity in the cargo holds as well as areas of the ship that aren't being used." She panned her audience. "That means your quarters when you're not in them. So secure your items."

When the others had left and Strand and Tommy had gone back to their stations, Dallas put her hand on Dana's arm. "What's going on?"

Dana glanced over to Strand. Strand met her eyes and gave a nod. "Sit down, Dallas. I've got a story you're not going to believe."

Chapter 36
Shock

To say that Dallas was stunned by what the captain had told her would be an understatement. An alternate universe? Of course, she'd heard of such things—in science fiction stories. At first, she thought Captain Stewart must be putting her on. But she had looked Dallas directly in the eye when telling her the story of the cave. And there was more. She and Strand had seen their doubles in the alternate timeline. On top of that, the captain had come back with healing powers and Strand with some kind of precognitive abilities. When Dallas insisted on proof of the captain's healing powers by making a small incision on her forearm and seeing it quickly heal into what looked like a scab that would have taken a day or two to form, Dallas was shocked. The captain then laughed and told her Strand and Wilson had both insisted on cutting themselves as well to prove she could heal them. So, Dallas wondered, but didn't ask, what other kinds of things could the captain heal? Could she heal chronic illnesses? Repair damaged organs? And she wondered what was going to happen to their ship that would require full power to the deflector shields? Strand didn't know. That was unsettling, but Dallas wasn't going to let herself worry about it. There was nothing she could do anyway.

As Dallas slowly walked to her quarters, which were behind the captain's on the same level as the bridge, she kept looking at her arm and pondering what the captain had told her. This alternate universe thing sounded so incredible in the sense of not being credible. No wonder the captain didn't want her uttering a word of it to anyone else.

Dallas waved her hand across her door and it slid open, sensing her unique energy signature. Stepping through the door, her thoughts were interrupted by an abrupt lack of gravity, and she grabbed a handrail to steady herself until the sensors recognized her presence and slowly turned on the gravity. Her feet drifted to the floor, and she regained her balance.

All of a sudden, Dallas felt tired. She took a deep breath then let it out with a whooshing sound. She pulled off her boots and padded to the facility. Examining herself in the mirror, she noticed faint dark circles under her eyes. Her short red hair was a bit unkempt, and her skin was pale. Maybe it was the light. Her skin always looked pale in this mirror.

While showering, she kept checking her arm. The scab had already disappeared and in its place was a faint white scar. Amazing, she thought. Not telling anyone else about this whole alternate universe business wouldn't be a problem. Who would she tell, anyway? The rest of the crewmembers were respectful but still distant with her, including Strand. The person she thought most likely to be distant with her, the captain, was actually the person closest to her now. Dallas would keep her word. She might have made mistakes in her life, but she valued her own integrity.

As she was drying herself off, Dallas noticed a small rash on her waist, just above her right hip. The skin had been sensitive in that area for several days, but she had ignored it. Well, she'd see Doc Sereno for the rash in a few days if it didn't disappear on its own. But right now, she needed some sleep.

Dallas slipped into her government issue PJs, which displayed the USSA logo, and she chuckled. Like anyone would care what she slept in. However, they were comfortable and sort of looked like hospital scrubs. Hers were a navy blue two-piece with short sleeves. The legs were a little short, but she didn't care. She was not as tall as Captain Stewart, but was a few inches taller than Echo Strand.

Just as she was easing herself into bed and pulling up the covers, the automated voice jolted her reverie. "Prepare for six-second hyper burst in five minutes." Damn. She hadn't bothered to check the schedule. She got up, pulled on her sweatshirt, also bearing the USSA logo, and strapped herself into her acceleration couch, opposite her bed. From this viewpoint, she could see through the three small portholes of her tiny quarters. But to get a better view, she snapped on the wallscreen just above her bed. Here we go, she thought, as the ship slowly accelerated then punched into full hyper. The stars streaked past as Dallas was pushed back into her couch. For some people, the experience was frightening, but for Dallas, it was a thrill. She watched the seconds count down on her wallscreen and then the ship slowed and the stars returned to normal. She waited for the all-clear signal from the computer voice, but it didn't come. Probably a glitch, she thought. She released her straps, but before she could get up, the ship went into a spin, knocking her to the floor and rolling her across the floor to her table, where she grasped its leg with both hands. But she couldn't hold on. She rolled across the small portholes, banging up her arms, and onto the ceiling, then crashed against the closet doors. The last thing she saw before the wallscreen hit her head was a white flash of light out of the portholes. Then everything went black.

Chapter 37
Fast Forward

When the ship stopped spinning, Echo took a few deep breaths to regain her bearings. Her stomach, however, was still rolling around inside her. Before she unbuckled herself, she instinctively reached into the leg pocket of her jumpsuit and fumbled around until she found her greengum. She quickly tossed two pieces into her mouth. As soon as she began to chew it, her stomach settled.

Nine acceleration cushions lined the circumference of the bridge. Only she, Tommy TwoTrees, and the captain were on the bridge at the time of the incident or whatever happened. The captain grabbed her comm from her shoulder and spoke into it.

"Everyone down there okay?" A few seconds passed before a reply came from Anderson.

"What the hell just happened?" He sounded angry and shocked.

"Don't know," said the captain. "How's our power? A few more seconds passed before Anderson spoke again.

"Down to minimum capacity, and our shield generators are fried."

TwoTrees interrupted. "Captain, this is really strange. You're not going to believe this."

"Try me," said the captain.

"We're only two point eight seven three hours from Atlantis Station at normal sublight speed."

The captain's seat belts clicked open, and she strode over to the nav station.

"I don't want to use up power by using the holo," TwoTrees explained. "Here, take a look at the screen."

Echo was curious and got up to look. TwoTrees pointed to a tiny blue planet in the distance.

The captain tapped her comm again. "Everyone come to the bridge now."

"How could that be?" said Echo. "We had over ten days to go."

"All I can think of is that vortex, or whatever it was, catapulted us forward on our journey," said TwoTrees.

The captain straightened up. "It's a good thing, I guess, since our power is so low."

Anderson, Mackovich, and Doc Sereno climbed up the stairs and entered the bridge.

"Where's Dallas?" the captain asked.

"I don't know," said Echo.

"Dallas, come in," said the captain. There was no answer. "Strand, go check her quarters."

Echo rushed to Dallas' door but it wouldn't open. She hurried back to the bridge. "Captain, I need you to override her lock."

The captain, Echo, and Doc Sereno found Dallas unconscious on the floor of her quarters, blood oozing from her right temple. Echo grabbed some gauze from the first aid kit and blotted the blood from her head. The doctor reached over and put his hand on her neck then listened to her breath. "She's alive. Bring in a stretcher and let's get her to the infirmary."

The captain spoke into her comm and in a few minutes, Anderson and Mackovich arrived with a portable stretcher. TwoTrees also came to observe. Everyone watched as Dallas was taken out of her room to the back of the ship where the small, two-bed infirmary was located.

"Mackovich, Anderson and Tommy. Thank you for your help. I'll let you know as soon as I find out anything. Tommy, I need you to mind the bridge and get us on course for Atlantis Station. Anderson, see what you can do to increase our power reserves—maybe collect some solar energy with our emergency array. Mackovich, check our cargo and make sure there's no damage to our hull, despite what our computer says or doesn't tell us. At this point, I don't trust it. Strand—" she trailed off as Echo's eyes locked with hers, silently asking to go with her and Doc to the infirmary. "Strand, you can come with us for now, but I want you back on that AI soon."

Echo breathed a sigh of relief and stood at the foot of the bed while the doctor revived Dallas with smelling salts. She winced at the strong ammonia odor, opened her eyes, then tried to sit up.

"Oh no you don't," said Doc as he gently pushed her shoulders back down. "You've got a nasty cut on your head."

The captain had already brought a cool damp cloth to the side of the bed and begun to apply it to Dallas' cut. She winced again. Echo watched with intense fascination as the captain placed a wad of sterile gauze over the wound and held her hand there for several minutes. When she removed the cloth, the wound had scabbed over.

"Strand, get me a Band-Aid."

Echo fumbled around in the drawers until she found what she was looking for, but Doc Sereno noticed the scab on Dallas' forehead before the captain could cover it up.

Dallas felt her scab with her fingers. "You're going to have to tell Doc," she said.

"Tell me what?"

Dallas glanced at the captain. "Well, I seem to have acquired a gift of sorts," said the captain.

"Please, enlighten me," said the doctor.

"I've got a rash on my waist. Maybe she can show you on that," said Dallas. Dallas tore open the Velcro on the right side of her jumpsuit.

The doctor examined it with interest. "Is your skin sensitive to the touch?"

"Yes, it has been for the last few days," said Dallas.

"If I didn't know any better, I'd say that's herpes zoster, otherwise known as shingles. Did you ever have chicken pox?"

Dallas thought for a moment. "As a matter of fact I did. My parents didn't have me vaccinated. They didn't believe in it."

"That's unfortunate," said the doctor.

Dallas frowned. "Well, they were against doctors, period." Dallas then closed the opening on her jumpsuit. "Go ahead, Captain. You won't have to put on any gloves if you do it through my clothing."

"I don't know if this is going to work. I've never attempted to heal a rash before." She placed her hands over Dallas' waist and held them there for a couple of minutes. "Okay, let's take a look now."

Doc Sereno looked on with amazement when Dallas exposed her waist to him again. The rash had completely disappeared. Only the skin was red where the rash had been. He gave the captain an inquiring look. "You may want to change careers, Dana. How did you do that?"

The captain put her hand on Doc's shoulder. "I'll tell you later," she said. "It's a long story."

"A story I would very much like to hear." He turned back to Dallas. "I'll give you a choice here. I can give you an injection now, or you can wait and see if our talented captain here can heal you. I would advise taking the injection. In most cases, taking the injection at the onset of the condition will prevent the post herpetic neuralgia."

"But the rash is gone."

"There's usually more to it than that."

"I never get sick. Ask anyone."

"This particular condition carries with it some serious nerve pain."

"I'm not feeling any pain."

"It usually starts a few days after the rash."

"I'll wait and see if I get it," said Dallas. "When can I get out of here?"

"Sit up slowly, then tell me how you feel."

"Fine," said Dallas, less than two seconds after she was in the sitting position, feet dangling from the side of the bed.

"No dizziness?"

"Nope."

Doc Sereno took her blood pressure. "It's a little high but not dangerously so, he said as he removed the cuff from her arm. "All right, but I want you to stay in your quarters until we reach the space station.

"The whole rest of the trip? You've got to be kidding."

Echo spoke up. "We're only," she looked at her wristcomm, "two point five three seven hours away from Atlantis. We may have gone through some kind of wormhole."

"So that's what it was?" Dallas slipped off the bed and searched for her boots. Echo brought them to her.

"We're not sure," said the captain. We had to reset our clocks."

"Interesting," said Dallas.

"Come on," said the captain. Strand and I will walk you back to your room."

Chapter 38
Waiting

As they neared the space station, Echo saw several craft lined up at each docking bay. They flew around the station, but all twenty bays had either spaceplanes or cargo ships waiting to be docked. Over the intercom, a female voice spoke: "Cargo ship *Sure Thing*, go to Loading

Dock Six and position yourself behind the cargo ship, *Pelican*. Wait time, approximately one point two hours."

"What's going on, Atlantis?" TwoTrees said.

"Have you not heard? Major quake in Southern California including Los Angeles County."

"We've received no such message," TwoTrees answered.

The captain stepped up to the viewscreen. "Visual please."

A female controller wearing a navy blue USSA uniform came into view. "*Sure Thing*, we lost your signal along the way." She consulted her computer. "We sent you a message at one zero-four-two-seven hours two days ago."

TwoTrees checked his nav computer, looked at the captain, then shook his head.

"Not received," said the captain. "We got sucked into some kind of vortex. Can you give us the correct date and time?"

"Say again, Captain?"

"We lost our chrono readings."

"Correct date is two-twelve-thirty. Standard orbit time is zero-niner-four-two."

The captain had a look of astonishment on her face but retained her composure. "Thank you, Atlantis. Proceeding to Loading Dock Six."

"Roger, Captain. Once you disembark and your manifest is checked, you will board the next available spaceplane for one of the nearest landing sites. USSA Southern California is shut down."

"Thank you, Atlantis. Stewart out."

Echo immediately thought of her mother and Jeremy, hoping they'd been spared from injury or death. Her heart raced, and anxiety overtook her body, as if it were instantly injected into every pore. It was a horrible feeling—being nervous not just mentally but physically. At her station on the bridge, she couldn't sit still. She wondered if the captain could calm her as she had done in the cave, but she didn't want to ask. The captain was busy and certainly concerned herself about the situation.

The waiting was difficult. None of them was allowed to make contact with Earth, as there were too many frequencies in use by the government, USSA, and the space stations. Not only had a 9.2

earthquake hit Southern California, but fierce Santa Ana winds blowing across the desert were wreaking havoc as well.

"Captain, may I go to my quarters?" Echo asked. At least there she could pace the floor and work out some of her nervous energy.

"Sure, Strand," she said without looking at Echo. Her eyes were fixed on the viewscreen, waiting for the departure of the next cargo ship to leave Bay 6.

In her tiny quarters, Echo stood in front of the full-length mirror that was attached to the outside of her facility door. She looked pale. At least her stomach wasn't upset. She hated when that happened. She sat down on her bed and took a few deep breaths. That helped. She was tempted to ask Doc for some anti-anxiety meds, but she didn't want to become dependent on them. Plus, she didn't want to appear weak—the request would permanently go on her USSA medical record. So she just sat and waited and breathed. To occupy her mind, she counted ten deep breaths, then paced the floor twenty times, then sat again and breathed deeply, alternating these activities. She couldn't concentrate on anything like reading, but she could practice some martial arts movements—not very extensively in her small space—but she did a few blocks and kicks in the stationary position.

Finally, she felt the ship move and heard the docking clamps attach with a dull thud. Her small bag of belongings was already packed, and she waited to hear the captain's order to disembark. Good-bye *Sure Thing*, she whispered.

Inside Atlantis, Echo and the rest of the crew watched as technicians reviewed *Sure Thing's* recording of its journey through the vortex. First, the familiar streak of stars filled the screen for several seconds. Then the ship returned to normal space. But a few seconds later, the ship began to spin, slowly at first, but then faster and faster. The stars became circular swirls and then the ship seemed to catapult forward at an incredible speed until it reached a pinpoint of light that grew larger as the ship slowed back into normal space. The ship was then sucked into the light hole and back out into black space within a matter of seconds. Echo remembered the ship filling with light so bright she had to cover her eyes.

"With that kind of propulsion, I'm surprised your ship survived," said one of the technicians.

The captain glanced at Echo but didn't let on that she had forewarning. "Our shield generator and deflector shields are no longer functional," she told the technician. "We used emergency backup and conservation to protect the ship the rest of the way back. But the ship will need a complete overhaul."

The technician eyed her for a moment but asked no further questions. "All right, Captain Stewart. You and your crew are dismissed. You'll need to go back to Bay Six and confirm your shipment."

As they left Operations, Echo took the captain aside. "Captain, I need to talk to you."

The captain looked at Echo with concern. "Of course. What's going on? Is it about the ship?"

"No, it's a personal matter."

The captain frowned for a split second and then spoke. "I still have to go over the manifest, but after that, how about I meet you in the crew lounge?"

"Thanks, Captain. I'll wait for you there."

The captain departed swiftly, and Echo strolled by the various kiosks in the public area of the space station, looking at merchandise without interest. Her mind was preoccupied with what she would say to the captain.

The USSA crew lounge was spacious with gray carpeting and muted blue walls. There was a small beverage and snack bar located to the left of the door as she entered. Several tables and chairs occupied one side of the lounge, while stuffed chairs and end tables were scattered on the other. Echo had been in here once before, before her first flight to Mars over two years ago. A quadruple-paned window showed a spectacular panoramic view of Earth from Atlantis' geosynchronous orbit. The lights in the lounge were dim for a better view, but tables and chairs had small reading lights.

Echo purchased a cup of ginger tea and made her way to one of the stuffed chairs at the far end of the room. Several people occupied the table area, and two others were sitting in the chair area. The room was relatively quiet, and Echo wished there was more ambient noise.

However, she believed her conversation with the captain would not be heard if she spoke softly.

Echo took a seat near the window and was awed by the view of Earth. But she kept glancing at her watch. She was still feeling nervous, but soon that would change, she hoped.

Forty-three minutes later, Captain Stewart strolled in. Dallas was behind her. They both ordered a drink and chatted for a moment. Then Dallas sat at one of the tables. Echo was relieved. She wanted to talk to the captain alone.

The captain came over to Echo and took a seat. "The manifest is accounted for, but it looks like we'll have a six-hour wait. They're sending us to Nellis Air Force Base."

Echo thought for a moment. That was in southern Nevada. They would probably be sent home by some kind of ground transportation or air train. Who knew how long that would take? "Have you heard from your daughter?"

"Yes, thankfully, she's still in New York with her father. Have you heard from your mother?"

"No. And they still won't let us comm to the greater Los Angeles area."

"Her store is out by Primeville, is that correct?"

"Yes."

"That's pretty far away from the epicenter, but I don't know about the winds."

"I just have to wait. I think she'll comm me. But that's not what I wanted to talk to you about, Captain."

The captain took a sip of her coffee and set it down on the end table that was between their chairs, which were perpendicular to each other. "What is it, Strand?"

"Well, it's partly about my job. I'm becoming weary of lengthy space travel. Plus, I feel like I need to learn something new."

"What do you want to do?"

"I don't know. I was thinking about becoming a spaceplane pilot. That way, I could go into space but wouldn't have to be cooped up in a ship for long periods of time."

"Or you can work in a different capacity at USSA or even go back to school. They'll help finance your education."

"I know. But there's a problem."

"Yes?" The captain's eyes were soft but concerned.

"I would have to quit your crew."

"You are a valuable member of my team, but I certainly would understand if you wanted to pursue a different career or further your education."

"Thank you, Captain."

The captain lifted her cup, took a sip of her coffee, and waited for Echo to continue.

"This is going to sound weird, but I just can't seem to stand being away from you for very long. When I woke up in Roy's house and everyone was gone, I feared the worst. And before that, when you were taken away by that, what do you call it?"

"Helicopter."

"I freaked. And when you flew to Canada with Dean and I couldn't go, I was worried the whole time. I guess in some way, I want to protect you, but it's because I can't stand the thought of losing you. It's for a selfish reason. And I feel like I am protected when you are with me. It doesn't make any sense."

The captain didn't say anything for what seemed like a long time. But she looked thoughtful as she stared out into space. Echo waited, wondering if there was anything the captain could say to ease her discomfort. Finally, the captain turned back toward her and spoke.

"When I was ten years old, my parents died. My grandmother raised Dean and me. My grandmother was a very kind woman and I adored her. But I didn't want to leave her side. I was afraid something would happen to her because of the trauma of losing my mom and dad. I didn't want to go to school, but of course I had to. I would rush home every day to make sure she was okay. I turned down invitations for sleepovers with friends and outings with children my own age, just so I could be with my grandmother as much as possible."

Echo thought she knew what was coming. The captain's grandmother probably forced her to go do other things. "So, how did you get over that fear?"

"My grandmother told me I could be with her as much as I liked, except for instances when we had to be apart, like when I went to school. She told me I would one day want to do things with other kids more than hang around the house with her. In other words, she let me play it out."

"Oh." Echo was surprised. "So how long did it take you to feel secure without being around her?"

The captain thought for a moment. "Mmm, two years, maybe a little longer. But my grandmother was a wise woman. She didn't push me away. She knew I would get over my need to protect her and my need for her to protect me. I finally got tired of following her around the house. One day the carnival came to town, and Grandma didn't want to go. One of my classmates invited me to go with her family. The thought of going on the rides and eating cotton candy and trying to win a stuffed animal by throwing darts at balloons intrigued me. I just couldn't stay away. So I accepted the invitation and thoroughly enjoyed myself. When I got back home that evening, Grandma was still there. Gradually, I went more and more places without her and learned to trust life."

"Is your grandmother still alive?"

"She passed away about five years ago, but by then, I could handle it. You've no doubt heard this before, but life usually doesn't hand us anything we can't handle."

"I just wanted you to know how I felt, Captain. I don't know that you can do anything about it."

"I'm glad you told me, and I pretty much already knew. What I'm saying is, you don't have to leave me or the crew. You can hang around me as long as you wish, but I believe you will, when you are ready, follow your own path. I don't think trying to separate yourself from me will help. It will only make matters worse if you are not ready. As for the protection part, it's an illusion to think any of us can protect one another. Your sense of feeling safe can only come from within here." She tapped Echo on the chest.

Echo felt her face flush as the truth of what the captain said struck her all at once. "Yeah, I guess I knew that."

"So, if you are tired of deep space travel, but your desire to stay with me is greater, then by all means you are welcome to stay on my crew. But at some point you may want to get some training in how to better use your precognitive abilities. That's quite a gift you acquired, Echo, and I think it can be developed to help others."

"You acquired a gift too, Captain."

"Yes, it is amazing. I'm not sure what to do with it. I don't want to be a professional healer. I like space, but I don't want to be stuck on a medical station either. I'm not a scientist."

Echo finished her tea. It seemed the conversation had come to an end. She looked over to the table area. Dallas was still there, reading. She glanced over at Echo and the captain.

"Maybe you should go talk to Dallas. I think she could use a friend right now."

Echo knew the crew had given her the cold shoulder, and Echo was not innocent of that behavior herself. As she and the captain approached the table where Dallas was sitting, Dallas suddenly doubled over in her chair.

"What's wrong?" said Echo.

"I don't know," Dallas managed to say. "Pain." People at neighboring tables began to stare.

"Can you walk?" asked the captain.

"I think so."

"Let's take you somewhere more private," said the captain.

With Echo supporting one side of Dallas and the captain supporting the other, they walked out of the lounge and headed for the infirmary.

Chapter 39
Pain

Dallas sat next to the window in the crowded spaceplane, Strand sat next to her, and a man from another crew sat next to Strand. Captain Stewart was in the aisle seat across the aisle and one row up from them. The injection Dallas had gotten at the infirmary on Atlantis had taken the edge off the pain, as had the captain's hand around her waist. However, neither of those treatments had permanently relieved the stabbing, burning sensation she was experiencing now.

"You should ask the captain to sit with you," Strand insisted.

"I can't bother her with this," said Dallas. "We'll land pretty soon and I'll get another shot."

"You're in pain. The captain can help. Why prolong your misery?"

"I should have taken the shot when Doc Sereno offered. He warned me."

"I'm going to get up and ask her. I'm sure she'll be happy to help." Strand started unbuckling herself, but Dallas tugged on her arm.

"Don't be foolish. It's dangerous to move about without any gravity. I can wait."

"Oh yeah, I forgot," said Strand.

It wasn't long before the spaceplane re-entered the Earth's atmosphere. Energy shields encapsulated the craft. An automated voice warned of turbulence and gravity. Dallas took a deep breath. The bumpy ride through the atmosphere was nothing compared to the pain in her waist. She just tried to breathe as deeply and evenly as possible.

When they landed, it took far too long for Dallas' turn to exit the spaceplane. Maybe if she got some ice it would help. While checking in at Customs, she asked where the infirmary was. The pain was unrelenting as she hurried along the lengthy concourse to the main terminal. Strand was trying to keep up with her, but got lost in the crowd. Dallas finally reached the urgent care clinic to find at least fifty air force uniformed patients waiting to be seen, along with a few USSA and civilian patients. She was told to take a seat. She asked for some ice, but none was available in the clinic. She left and found a water machine that dispensed ice chips. She removed a bandana from her duffel and filled it with a healthy amount of ice. Two other people were waiting for water and must have thought she was odd for taking so much ice, but she didn't care. Immediately, she ripped open the side of her jumpsuit and applied the ice, holding it there as she made her way back to the clinic. When she entered the clinic, she found Strand and Captain Stewart waiting for her.

"Let the captain help you," Strand said.

Dallas took a seat between them. "I don't know how much it will help. The last time she helped, the effects wore off pretty fast."

"So, she can alleviate the pain while you are waiting."

Dallas looked at Captain Stewart and gave her a nod. After removing the ice, Dallas let the captain place one hand on her exposed waist. She was expecting to feel heat as she had the last time the captain had placed her hand on her, but what she felt was pleasantly cool, even after the ice. The captain held her hand on Dallas' waist for at least five minutes, and the pain faded significantly. The captain removed her hand and asked her how she felt.

"Much better, but I don't know how long it will last."

"Let's wait and see," said the captain.

After about ten minutes, Dallas felt the pain returning. At first it was a burning sensation followed by the more intense stabbing sensation. Dallas decided to put her own hand over the area, and to her surprise, the stabbing sensation diminished, but not as much as it had when Captain Stewart had used her hand. So the captain continued to hold her hand over the area until Dallas was finally called in to see a doctor. Strand and Captain Stewart stayed in the waiting room.

"Nerve pain is very difficult to get rid of," said the doctor, an older woman wearing air force scrubs. "If you would have taken the injection at the time of the onset of the rash, or even before that, you would have been spared most of the pain."

"How long is this going to last?"

"It's different with everyone. For some it's a few weeks. For others it can be years."

"Years!" said Dallas, alarmed. That was ridiculous. Dallas wasn't going to allow herself to be disabled for years. Her parents had taught her the mind can heal the body. That was why they were so against doctors and drugs. But for now, her mind was just not strong enough. The pain was just too "loud."

"No good will come from worrying about it. Shingles is brought on by stress or a weak immune system and usually attacks people much older than you. Since you are in your thirties, I would predict you will heal sooner than later. But you need to take measures to relax. I can give you some tablets that will take the edge off the pain, but you need to take it easy for a while. You can also continue to apply ice and take hot baths. The contrast between heat and cold will help."

"Thank you, Doctor." Dallas hopped off the examination table and got dressed.

"The pharmacy is just outside the clinic, around to your left."

Dallas emerged from the doctor's office and told Strand and Captain Stewart she was going to the pharmacy. They followed her.

Once she had her prescription, the three of them met up with the rest of the crew in an area reserved for USSA personnel.

Inside the windowless room, a large wallscreen showed live images of the earthquake damage in Southern California. Hovercraft transmitted aerial views while local cameras captured damaged buildings and highways. Momentarily, a USSA spokeswoman entered the room and the ambient chatter ceased.

"I know you all are eager to get home. We are doing our best to transport as many people as possible to their destinations. However, buses and air trains are filled to capacity. As you may have seen on the news, the Southern California USSA runways are damaged." Dallas looked up at the wallscreen waiting for images of the USSA base. On the eight-way split screen, many images kept repeating, but in the far lower right portion of the screen, she saw the buckled pavement of the USSA runways. She gasped.

"You people who live in the greater Los Angeles area will be sent to LAX either by conventional aircraft or to L.A. by air train. However, because of the need, medical personnel will be sent first. We have no facilities for keeping any of you all night, so we will try and get you out by the end of the day. Now, please raise your hands if you are medically trained."

Dallas had taken a first aid class years ago, but she wasn't that eager to get home. Besides, she was not feeling well herself, so she didn't feel up to helping others. However, Doc Sereno and Captain Stewart raised their hands. She wondered if Stewart was going to reveal her secret abilities. In the meantime, Strand's comm buzzed and she left the room to take her call. Dallas didn't care who did what as long as the pain didn't return in full force. Her parents wouldn't approve, but she was going to use the pills she got from the pharmacy, despite the long list of side effects that popped out as a holo when she touched the name of her medication on the pill bottle.

Medical personnel were asked to come to the front of the room, and the rest of the group was dismissed to use a limited number of shops and restaurants at the air force base. They were told their individual names would be called and they would be told where to assemble when a mode of transportation was ready to take them to Southern California.

Dallas picked up her duffel and waited in line to exit the crowded room. As she went out the door and into the hallway, she saw Strand and Stewart in a serious interchange. Strand looked upset. Dallas overheard Stewart telling Strand that she felt a responsibility to go help the earthquake victims. Strand looked as if she were going to protest. Her face was flushed and she seemed to be holding back anger. Dallas decided to intervene.

"Echo, why don't we go get something to drink," Dallas said. Captain Stewart gave her a look that said, thank you.

Strand swallowed. "Sure."

"I'll see you both back in Los Angeles. I'm not sure when. Maybe in a few days," said the captain.

"Right," said Dallas. Dallas gently took Strand by the arm and turned her away from Stewart. "C'mon, I hear this place has a lounge with a great view of the runway."

Strand said nothing as she and Dallas headed down the concourse toward the elevator that would take them to their destination.

The officer's lounge was located on the third and top floor of the main terminal building. It was not as luxurious as the USSA lounge on Atlantis Station, but it offered a wider variety of food and drink, including beer, wine, and hard liquor. Strand and Dallas chose a small circular table close to the window.

"So, have you heard from your mother?" Dallas asked when they were both seated.

"Yes, she's okay. Only a small amount of damage to her grocery store, but nothing that will cost her much. That's what she said anyway."

A young man came to their table to take their order. "I'll have a ginger ale," said Dallas. She wasn't supposed to drink any alcohol with the pills she was taking.

"Nothing for me," Strand said.

"Why don't you try a beer?" Dallas suggested.

Strand shrugged. "Okay."

"Bring a draft, please" Dallas told the waiter. The flush in Echo's face had diminished, but it looked to Dallas as if she were carrying a lot of anger. "Are you mad at me?"

The question seemed to take Strand by surprise. "No, of course not. Why do you ask?"

"Well, on the ship, you didn't talk to me much. I was wondering if you were okay with me being the XO."

Strand shrugged again. "I guess."

The young man brought their drinks and left. "I know you've been with the Stewart crew much longer than I have."

Strand took a sip of her beer. "Wow, this has a bite. I haven't had a beer in quite a while. Personally, I like marijuana better."

Dallas laughed, glad that Strand had broken the ice, so to speak. "Well I hope the beer relaxes you."

Strand seemed to become defensive again. "I can relax without it."

"Okay." Dallas didn't want to upset her.

Strand gulped down half the glass of brew. Dallas didn't say anything.

After a few minutes, Strand stood up. Her face was flushed again. "I don't feel so well. I'm going to the facility."

"Want me to come with you?"

"No thanks."

Dallas waited for Strand to return, but after about fifteen minutes, she went looking for the young woman. She ducked into two different multi-facilities and called out for Echo, but there was no response. Then she found a single unit facility, but the door was locked. She stood outside and waited for some time between five and ten minutes, but no one came out, so she knocked. Her waist was beginning to burn again, but she ignored it.

"Strand. Echo. Are you in there?" She didn't yell so loud as to attract attention. Finally, she heard the door unlatch. Dallas opened it to find Strand sitting on the floor in the corner near the toilet. Her face was red and wet from crying, but she didn't make a sound, nor did she look at Dallas.

Dallas locked the door and approached Strand. "What's going on?"

Strand made a half-turn toward the wall. "Stay away," she said in a muffled voice.

"Strand, I'm not going to leave you alone until you tell me what's going on." Dallas extended her hand. "At least stand up. You can't stay in here forever."

Strand didn't take Dallas' hand, but she stood up. Dallas, in her boldness, put her arms around Strand from behind. Strand tried to wiggle out of her grasp, but Dallas only held on tighter. Finally, Strand went limp in her arms and let out a few quiet sobs. When Dallas was satisfied that Strand would not try and get away, she slowly loosened her hold on her. Dallas slowly turned Strand toward her so that they were face-to-face. Her eyes were puffy and her nose was red. Dallas grabbed some toilet tissue and stuffed it into Strand's hand. Strand blew her nose, then ran the tap, splashing water on her face.

"It's Captain Stewart, isn't it?" Dallas said while Strand was drying her face and hands.

"What?" Strand acted surprised, but Dallas could tell her question had struck a chord.

"The reason you're upset," said Dallas.

Strand swallowed then blew her nose again. "I suppose it is," she said.

"Are you sensing any danger?"

Strand took a deep breath and let it out in a sigh. "No."

"Well?"

"I'm sorry, Dallas. I don't know what's gotten into me. I'm just worried about her all the time, especially when she's not with me."

"Oh, I see." Dallas didn't "see," but she went along with whatever might calm Strand. "She'll be okay. She can take care of herself."

"I know."

"You miss her, don't you?"

Strand nodded. "I do."

Dallas sensed she should change the subject, get Strand out of there. "Come on, let's wander around this place. I hear they have a museum somewhere on this base."

"Sure, okay." They exited the facility and headed toward the directory in the hallway. "I forgot to ask you how you're feeling," said Strand.

The burning sensation in her side had switched to a stabbing pain, but it was dulled by the medicine. "I'll be okay," said Dallas. She hoped that was the case.

Chapter 40
Collateral Damage

The network of orbiting solar power satellites continued to beam energy to the Earth-based receiving stations, the rectennas, in various areas around the globe. North America had eleven such receiving stations. The closest one to California was just north of Nellis AFB in the Nevada desert. It spanned a little over twenty-two square kilometers and served the western United States. Transmission lines from the station were buried, so the Santa Anas didn't blow them down. However, some of the lines had been damaged by the earthquake and its aftershocks resulting in large areas of California being without power.

Dana arrived in Los Angeles on an overcrowded air train. From the elevated train, she could see damage to highways, buildings, and structures. Air taxis were busy, and she had to wait for over an hour to catch one to her house. Doc Sereno accompanied her on the air train, but they parted ways at the train station so he could check on his family. The plan was for them to meet up at one of the Red Cross stations. Now that he knew about her healing powers, she could follow him, helping victims who needed bleeding stopped and possibly bones set and mended. She was soon to find out the extent of her abilities.

The area where Dana lived was without grid power for several kilometers. Her house had its own generator, powered by rooftop solar panels in combination with hydrogen fuel cells. Because of the built-in seismic bracing in her house, there was only minimal damage, most of it inside. Several wall paintings had fallen to the floor or become askew, and a floor lamp had tipped over. The few books she had on her bed's headboard had fallen from their case onto her bed. The winds had blown out some of the photovoltaic cells on the roof, but there were still enough to power the generator.

Instead of venturing out again, she commed the Red Cross and asked them and Doc Sereno to meet at her house, which she offered as a temporary shelter and medical clinic. In less than an hour, medical personnel and volunteers brought in cots and supplies. As victims were brought into her house, Dana thought about the destruction she'd seen from the air taxi. Some portions of the city appeared untouched by damage, while other areas had crumbled bricks and buckled streets. Energy bands that powered vehicles along freeways had been disrupted in many places by the power outages. Although it had been three days since the major quake, tremors still followed. It was unnerving every time one hit. Sometimes they came in the middle of transporting a patient from an ambulance into the house. Other times, a tremor would shake the house while Dana was bandaging a patient.

Most the time, she spent applying pressure bandages, making sure she held her hand over the wound until the bleeding stopped, or until she sensed it had stopped. She was picking up some deeper intuition like Strand had acquired. So far, as far as she knew, no one suspected her healing abilities.

After several hours, Dana had run out of rooms to put people. When a young patient was carried in by stretcher, the Red Cross organizers and triage nurses directed the patient be set on some cushions on the floor in the hallway just outside the kitchen. Her thigh was crushed, and she had a dislocated hip. She had been sedated with morphine. Dana didn't know if she could heal broken bones, but she was willing to give it a try. She knelt down and lightly placed one hand on the girl's thigh while placing the other on her hip. People scurried by her in the hallway, not taking the time to ask her what she was doing. Doc Sereno was standing nearby, waiting for her to finish her treatment. When Dana sensed the girl had enough, she removed her hands. Doc Sereno then scanned her with a portable imaging device. The bone had been healed, but the hip would need to be set back into place.

"Might as well do it while she's still sedated," Doc said.

Dana moved out of the way. "I don't know if I did any good as far as the pain goes," said Dana. At least the leg is okay. Does anyone know what happened to her?"

"Someone might. She was probably crushed by something inside a building."

Doc Sereno set her hip while Dana held her breath. The girl yelped and opened her eyes. Dana had hardly looked at her face before, but now she did a double take. The girl was Lucy. Lucy from the cave. Lucy who'd gone to the alternate universe with her. Lucy who was supposed to have gone back to Mexico.

"Captain Dana?" the girl said in a weak voice.

"Yes, it's me, Lucy. Don't try to talk."

"It hurts. Please make the pain go away."

Doc Sereno stepped in to give her more morphine, but Dana stopped him. "Let me try something first," she said. Dana lightly placed one hand on Lucy's hip and the other on her thigh.

Lucy flinched. "Just take a few deep breaths, Lucy, and let me know if the pain is going away."

Lucy did as she was told. Dana felt the girl's body relax as she held her hands over the painful areas. What was new to Dana, was she began to feel the girl's nerves and muscles as if her hands were inside. The muscles relaxed as the nerves calmed. "How do you feel now?" Dana asked.

"Better. You made me better just like when we were in the cave."

Dana turned to Doc Sereno. "Let's put her in my bed."

"I thought you wanted to reserve that space for yourself. You'll need to rest soon, Captain."

"I know, but if need be, I'll share the bed with her. I know this girl."

"Okay. Let's move her onto a stretcher and take her upstairs."

Once Lucy was settled in bed, Dana started to leave, but Lucy grabbed her arm. "I'm sorry I lied to you, Captain Dana."

Dana sat down on the edge of the bed. "You can just call me Dana. What do you mean, Lucy?"

"I told you my parents and I snuck over the border."

"Yes?"

"It was me. Only me. I ran away."

Chapter 41
Lucy

It had been close to a month, and the pain was nearly gone. At first, Dallas had taken Captain Stewart up on her offer of hands-on healing to temporarily alleviate the pain from time to time. She had stopped taking the pain pills some time ago. She was not going to let this nerve pain get her down. She had about three bad days there, but after that, Dallas' condition improved. She had asked the captain what she felt and what she was thinking when she used her hands for healing. The captain had told her it was different for everyone, but that basically, she could feel energy moving from her hands into the person, and could also feel energy coming out of the person. Her hands would pull the disruptive energy out of the person and then she would shake her hands out. She told the patient to breathe into the area. But the thing that really seemed to help patients was if she could make a heart connection with them. Dallas didn't really understand all this—the mechanics of it maybe—because she hadn't experienced it. But she had decided to try it on herself. Each day and evening, she sat or lay down with her hand over her waist. She imagined she was breathing into the affected area. She did it for at least twenty minutes at a time. It calmed her and did ease the pain.

Dallas was just getting up from the couch, when Captain Stewart entered the den (the door was open). "Are you doing okay?"

"Yeah," said Dallas as she righted herself on the couch. "What's up?"

"Lucy's asking for you."

"Okay. Tell her I'll be there in a few minutes." Since the earthquake, Captain Stewart had taken custody of Lucy. Also, during that time, Dallas had reluctantly accepted the captain's offer to stay with her, since the Southern California USSA base was being shut down, and that's where Dallas had been living. As for Strand, she had gone to live with her mother and work in her grocery store. Both the captain and Dallas had contacted her by comm early on, but Echo Strand had seemed distant and hadn't contacted either one of them since. That was about three weeks ago. The Southern California USSA crews were on furlough until accommodations for more spacecraft could be assimilated into other bases. And, Coop Wilson was home.

Dallas still felt a bit uncomfortable living here, especially with Wilson home. She liked him okay, but she felt out of place with the captain and Wilson being a couple and all. Helping Lucy with her schoolwork and taking her on outings made her feel needed, and the captain *was* giving her free room and board. But as soon as she saved up enough money, she was going to get her own place or one with Echo, if Echo still wanted to room together. Not knowing where her crew would be stationed was also something she'd like to know before investing in an apartment. At least that pesky shingles virus had pretty much healed.

Dallas tapped lightly on Lucy's bedroom door. "Enter," she heard Lucy say.

Lucy was zeroed into a small transparent screen that hovered just above her bed. "Hey Dallas. Can you help me with my math?"

"Maybe." Dallas sat down on the edge of the bed, clearing a spot to sit. Lucy's room was cluttered with real books, electronic tablets, stuffed animals, clean clothes, dirty clothes, shoes, a tennis racket, and a basketball among other things. Dallas hadn't been an "A" student in school, but she had always been good with math. When Lucy needed her help, Dallas would often have to look up a formula, but it would come back to her easily.

After they'd gone through a few math problems, Lucy stopped, and looked at Dallas with her big round eyes. "Do you think Dana will be able to keep me?"

"I don't know, Lucy. I certainly hope so, if that's what you want."

"Of course it's what I want. Any kid living in an orphanage wants to be adopted, especially if they are leaving Mexico for America."

"Well, I don't see any reason why she wouldn't be able to keep you."

Lucy hung her head. "Yeah, but it's the waiting I don't like." Then she looked at Dallas again. "My mom and dad said if I ever got the chance, I should live in America."

It must be awful to lose your parents at so young an age, Dallas thought. Captain Stewart had told her that Lucy's parents had been killed in a car accident when Lucy was only four years old. She had lived in an orphanage ever since. Most people wanted to adopt younger children, so Lucy had one day decided to run away.

"Do you have a mom and dad?" Lucy asked her out of the blue.

"Uh, yeah. They live back East—New York."

"Do you ever visit them?"

"Not for a long time. They're pretty busy." Dallas tried to think of the last time she'd talked to her parents. Several months ago, she guessed. They'd talked by comm. Her mother had asked Dallas to come and visit, but Dallas didn't think she really meant it. Her mother worked at an art gallery and was scheduled solid with events and social activities. Her father was a banker and had had to start over when the president reset the economy, but he wasted no time accumulating accounts. She was sure they both loved her, but they were involved in their own lives.

"Well, if my mom and dad were alive, and I were an adult, I'd go visit them as much as I could."

Dallas felt sympathy for the girl. "I bet you would."

"Anyway, Dana and Coop have to go to Mexico to finalize the adoption."

"You must feel very good about that."

"They're taking me with them."

"So when are you leaving?" Dallas thought that when they were gone, it would be a good time for her to move out. She was back working at her nuclear waste disposal job, except that now the containers had to be trucked out of the base to a rocket launching facility in New Mexico. If she could get a couple of co-workers to help her move on their days off, she could probably get it done in a day. She didn't have much, and some of her stuff was still at the base. Some of the buildings had collapsed, but her quarters had pretty much remained intact. However, to be safe, all the buildings on the base were going to be torn down. At the time the base was built, the government didn't have the finances to make it structurally sound in case of an earthquake. As for the crippled runways, they would probably stay as is until or if someone wanted to use the land for something else. Dallas wondered how they were going to get the grounded spaceplanes out of there. Maybe disassemble them and truck them out like the nuclear waste? There wasn't any way any kind of aircraft was going to take off from that base. And LAX couldn't accommodate the huge spaceplanes, which needed very long runways.

Lucy shrugged. "Not sure. They are waiting to hear from the people who will let them adopt me."

"You're lucky, kid."

"I know."

Dallas stood up. "So, are we done here for now?"

"Yeah, I guess. I want to comm some of my friends."

"When your schoolwork is all done."

"It is—what's due tomorrow anyway."

"Okay. I'll talk to you later, kid." Dallas was partway through the door when Lucy called back to her.

"Dallas?"

Dallas turned on her heal. "Yes?"

"I wish you would stay living with us."

"I promise I'll come and visit."

"You promise?"

Dallas smiled. "Yes, Lucy, I promise."

Chapter 42
Mexico

Dana, Coop, and Lucy got out of the taxi, opened the chain link fence gate, and walked up the cement walkway to the large house where Lucy had lived most of her life. It was easy to see why this place could have been mistaken for a regular home and not an orphanage. A large swing set was set up on the left side of the house and a sandbox could be seen nearby. When Jamey and Amando had dropped Lucy off here, the man and woman who ran the place told them, yes, Lucy lived here, and they had been worried about her. Amando had assumed they were her parents.

Children played in the spacious dirt yard while chickens and dogs ran free among them. The fence was about six feet high, slightly taller than Dana. She had asked Lucy several times why she had run away, but Lucy only answered that her parents had told her to go live in America if she ever got the chance. Dana was sure her parents didn't mean for her to do that when she was only twelve years old.

They were greeted at the front door by the foster parents, who spoke a limited amount of English. As Coop, Lucy, and Dana were escorted into the dining room, Dana noticed a large Christian cross prominently displayed in the common room.

"Please sit," said Mrs. Valdez. Mr. Valdez shook hands with Coop and Dana, and they all sat down at a large dining room table. The couple shared the same last name, so they were obviously old-fashioned in that regard. Dana guessed the wife had taken her husband's last name.

"How many children live here?" Dana asked.

Lucy translated Dana's question into Spanish and Mrs. Valdez's answer into English. "Fourteen, but it varies. Sometimes there are as few as ten, but then new kids come too."

Mr. Valdez had a better command of English, so he started the questioning. "We are glad you want to adopt Lucy. But we are concerned that she ran away."

"We are too," said Coop. "Without meaning to offend," he continued, "are the children well cared for here?"

Mr. Valdez's face became serious. "Of course."

Coop looked at Lucy for confirmation. "He is correct."

"Then why would you run away?" said Coop. "And I want more of a reason than your parents told you to go to America if you got the chance."

Lucy looked away. Dana gently touched her face and turned it back toward her. Lucy took a deep breath. "This sounds stupid and you won't believe me."

"Try us," said Coop. All four adults' eyes were on her now.

"I just thought I could find someone who would feel sorry for me and take me in. Someone who would give me my own room and send me to a good school."

"So that's it?" said Mr. Valdez. "You put your life in danger by hitching rides across the border and going all the way to the California mountains?"

"Someone good found me, didn't they?" said Lucy defensively.

"Yes, and someone bad could have found you too."

Lucy hung her head. "I know."

"So how do I know you won't run away from these nice people here?"

"I'd never want to run away from them."

Dana's heart melted a little bit on hearing that. However, she still wished that Lucy would be more open with her. She hadn't told her exactly how she got across the border, and she had lied about living with her mother and father.

Mr. Valdez skimmed through the literature he had in front of him. "You both are spaceship captains, I see. What will Lucy do when you are away from Earth?"

Coop spoke up. "She can go with one of us if she wants. But most the time one of us will be home with her."

"Your space agency allows you to bring your children along on your trips?"

"Yes, most the time," Dana answered. "I brought my daughter with me to Mars, and one of my crewmembers brought her adopted son along." She remembered how Mackovich had taken to David Lee, who was left orphaned after his father was killed in a skirmish on the solar power station when the government and the corporations were at war.

"And your daughter," said Mrs. Valdez. "Why does she not live with you?"

"Cheyenne has chosen to live with her father because they share the same interests. But we keep in touch."

"There is another thing we would like you to do," said Mr. Valdez.

Dana and Coop looked at each other then back at the couple. "Yes?" Dana answered.

"We will give Lucy over to you, but we prefer that you are married."

That was a surprise. "Uh, well is that required for the adoption?" said Dana.

When neither Valdez answered, Lucy asked them the question in Spanish.

"We would prefer it," said Mr. Valdez.

"In our culture, we have many single parents and domestic partners that are not married," said Coop. "But," he turned to Dana, "I would be willing if you would."

Dana thought for a moment. What would it hurt? They could always dissolve the marriage if it didn't work out, and they should still be able to keep Lucy. "Okay, we can sign an agreement to be married. But it's not going to be today. Let me see the contract." She searched any wording that would require Lucy to be returned to the orphanage if the marriage dissolved, but she found no such wording. The adoption would be final once both parties signed.

After both parties reviewed the contract, the Valdez's agreed to the adoption. However they required a substantial "donation" to the orphanage. Dana had expected that. When she pulled out two bars of uzerium, she wished she had a photo of the surprised looks on their faces. Dana had to refrain from snickering. Money surely did talk in certain circumstances—uzerium even more.

It was obvious that Lucy had no great affection for the Valdez's. What she probably missed most was the personal attention and care that real parents would give her, but she was unable to express that desire. That's what Dana guessed anyway. The orphanage seemed neat and clean, and the children seemed content.

As they stepped out the front door, Lucy was greeted by a little boy, not more than six years of age. Lucy knelt down to him and spoke something to him in Spanish. The boy's eyes teared up, and Lucy gave him a hug. The boy clung to her, and she had to gently push him away while still holding him by the shoulders. "Eres joven. Tu serás adoptado, Héctor. Sigue siendo un bueno chico para mi. Bien?" Lucy then turned to Dana and Coop. "I told him he is young and will be adopted and to keep being a good boy for me." Héctor nodded and wiped the tears from his eyes.

On the way out, Dana noticed a large building in back of the house. "What's in there?" she asked Lucy.

"Um, that's where we have school." The girl's face betrayed her lie.

Dana stopped at the end of the walkway. "Lucy, tell me the truth."

Lucy sighed. "Well, the younger kids do have school, but the older kids learn how to sew."

"I see. And do they get paid for it?"

"Mr. and Mrs. Valdez said we have to earn our own way once we reach twelve years of age."

"I see." Dana wanted to go in and expose them for child labor. It wasn't right, but it also wasn't her country. There was nothing she could do about it.

So, Dana had more clues as to why Lucy had run away. She believed she was too old to be adopted, and she was put to work when she turned twelve. In another six years, she would be on her own, with minimal skills and no opportunity for college. And she'd be living in a country that, while it had made great economic progress in the last hundred years, still presented few opportunities to make a good living. Lucy was smart. Dana could tell by how well she was doing in school.

And she was eager to learn, not putting off doing her homework like many kids did. They would have to work on her trust issues though. Lucy was still secretive and was reluctant to share her experiences with Dana. But if anyone could gain her trust, it was Dana.

On the train ride back to California, Dana thought about settling down and having a real family that was together all the time. Perhaps she could limit her flights to four per year rather than ten or twelve. And marriage. Dana had told Cheyenne she and Coop were going to try and adopt Lucy. Cheyenne seemed okay with that, still preoccupied with making movies with her father. But Dana wondered how Cheyenne would react to Coop and her getting married. Kids were funny that way. Even though their parents were divorced, many children still held hope they would get back together. Dana had told Cheyenne there was no way she and Ben would remarry. Cheyenne liked Coop, but what would she think of him as a stepfather? Dana contemplated these thoughts as Lucy slept with her head on Dana's shoulder. In the seat in front of them, Coop was quiet all the way home.

Chapter 43
Echo's Answer

"I wish you wouldn't go to that cave again," Eudora said as Echo was packing her duffel.

"I'll be okay."

"As much as I've enjoyed having you here with me these last few weeks, I really think you need to go back to your captain and your friends."

"I'm not ready yet," said Echo. Eudora had obviously noticed her despondency. Echo had not been very enthusiastic about working at the store. But she just had to get away from the captain. She hated her need to be with her all the time. Despite what the captain had told her, Echo believed the only way she could get over that need was to separate herself from the captain and everyone associated with her. She wasn't in love with Captain Stewart. She knew that. She was happy that the captain and Wilson were a couple. But what was similar to being in love was the longing Echo felt to be near her captain. She hated herself for feeling that way. But the separation had not eased her feelings; it had only intensified them. So maybe she could find some answers if she went to the cave and the American Indian medicine woman appeared to her again.

"At least comm me when you get there," Eudora said.

"Okay, will do." Echo finished packing and put her bedding and food into her small vehicle, which she drove to LAX. It was nice not to have to wear a breather while outside in the greater Los Angeles area. Since the USSA base had shut down, air pollution had decreased in the city by over eighty percent, or so said the news reports. Airplanes used synthetic fuels, which still polluted the air somewhat, but nothing like the propellants that fueled the spaceplanes. Well, the pollution would just go somewhere else, but not having to use a breather in Los Angeles was a blessing.

The flight to Spike took less than thirty minutes. As she had before, Echo rented a Jeeper Creeper for the drive to the cave that sat off a narrow dirt road on a cliff in the high desert. It was the beginning of spring, and on her way, she noticed a few cacti in bloom. The air was clear and thin, and Echo took a deep breath as she exited the cave after parking her vehicle inside. It was late afternoon, and Echo didn't feel like settling down yet, so she took a walk down the road and commed her mother to tell her she had arrived and was okay. With that out of the way, she returned to the cave, seeing only two vehicles pass her by.

Once Echo had set up her bedding on the precipice where she had slept before, she threw a lightweight blanket around her shoulders, sat on her bedding, and leaned against the cave wall. Once she closed her eyes to meditate, she felt lonelier than the last time she was here. As before, she longed for the companionship of the group she had first come here with—Amando, Jamey, Lucy, Dean, and of course, the captain. She felt tears well up in her eyes and took a few deep breaths. Why was she trying to hold the tears back? There was no one here to see her cry. Maybe she was afraid that if she started, she would not be able to stop. After a few minutes, though, she was unable to hold back the flood of sadness that enveloped her, and she lay down on her bedding, with her head sunk into her pillow, and sobbed.

Echo didn't know how much time had passed until she checked her watch. She had lain here for almost two hours. The sun was low in the sky, and the cave was getting dark. She sat up and took a drink of water from her canteen. Then she went into the facility, which, to her delight, was still operational, and she splashed some water on her face. It was cold, and she shivered. Back outside the facility, she quickly set out some heat globes and built herself a small fire in the pit with some kindling she had brought with her from Spike. But she wasn't hungry yet. She was still too upset to eat.

"Why do I feel so bad?" she asked whatever spirits occupied the cave, but she got no answer. She sat for a long time in front of the fire, hoping to hear an answer. But no American Indian medicine woman appeared. Nor did a fairy godmother or angel answer her. There was only the snapping and popping of the fire, slowly dying out, and the sound of her own ragged breathing.

Echo dowsed the fire and climbed into her sleeping bag. She was exhausted from her emotional upset, and fell asleep soon after her head touched her pillow. She woke once, briefly, at the sound of a vehicle driving by, but then she fell into a sound sleep.

Her first dream was disturbing. It seemed as if she were watching a movie, but she was also a character in the movie, a soldier in a firefight, running for a foxhole. A group of soldiers dressed in olive drab with matching helmets were running and shooting at other soldiers who were similarly dressed. The enemy soldiers were shooting from positions inside semi-destroyed stone buildings. Echo's team was advancing on them, trying to take over what appeared to be a small town in mid-twentieth century Europe. Echo was a male soldier as were the others in her company. The leader yelled, "Go." The soldier that Echo saw herself as ran with her rifle for the next foxhole just as a barrage of machine gun fire was coming her way. Another soldier, who she assumed was her best friend in this firefight, flung himself on top of the Echo soldier throwing both of them out of the line of fire, thus saving the Echo soldier's life. Echo woke abruptly and sat up. The dream was so poignant. She closed her eyes and tried to remember the details. After reviewing the dream, she knew without a doubt that the soldier who had saved her life was the captain.

Hunger pangs interrupted Echo's thoughts. She dug into her duffel and took out a sandwich. The bread was a bit dry, but the cheese and meat inside tasted fresh. She wanted something hot to drink, but didn't feel like making another fire, so she settled for water. After using the facility, she came back to her bed and sat for a long time, staring at the carvings on the cave wall. She was just about to lie down again, when she saw a vision on the cave wall.

At first, the picture was still. It looked like a painting and showed soldiers on horses battling with spears, shields, and crossbows. The men riding the horses were dressed in ancient garb like those of the Roman Empire in its height. Helmets consisted of close fitting metal caps, some with nose guards. Men wore skirts with knee high boots. Opponents rode camels and wore headdresses on their helmets. The poor animals they were riding were reared up on their hind feet. Echo gasped as the picture came to life. Again, she found a soldier she felt was herself, perhaps in another lifetime. Fortunately, she was spared the sounds of the battle, just as she had been in the dream. An opponent was just about to stab a spear into the soldier next to her, but the Echo soldier jumped off her horse and grabbed the soldier, saving that soldier's life. Except this time, the Echo soldier was fatally stabbed and fell to the ground. She watched with horror as horses trampled her/his already dead body. However, the soldier whose life she saved rode off with his companions after their enemy retreated. The picture then faded from the cave wall. Somehow, Echo knew she had saved the captain's life. Echo lay back down and stared out into the spacious cave until her eyes finally closed and she fell back to sleep.

Just before dawn, she had another dream. This one was very bizarre, as it didn't seem to fit any time in history. She was on the bridge of a spaceship with the captain and her crew, but they were animated characters, as if they were players in a video game. They were out in space shooting at and receiving fire from another spacecraft. Flanked around them were escort ships, some of which took fatal hits. Echo didn't know what the war was about, only that it had been going on for a long time. Her ship was badly damaged and shields were down to twenty percent. Missiles were coming at them in all directions. And then, when she thought conditions could not get any worse, her ship took one huge hit and exploded. Everyone on board was killed. That saddened Echo, though she was still an observer, thus she must be alive. But then the game started all over again, and her crew sat unharmed on a fresh new ship.

Echo sat up and rocked back and forth to warm herself. Although the dreams and visions had shown her why she wanted to protect her captain so much, and perhaps why she felt protected in her presence, they hadn't revealed to her how she might be free of needing to be with the captain.

Frustrated, Echo packed up her things and drove back to Spike to board the next flight to LAX. But on the crowded flight, a realization came to her, and her own inner voice told her to go back to the captain. That she was not yet ready to strike out on her own, and that the captain and the rest of her crew and friends needed her as much as she needed them. And when the time came for her to leave the captain, she would be ready.

By the time Echo was driving back to her mother's house, she felt a calm peace come over her. Why had she been fighting her own destiny? But her peace was interrupted by her sudden urgency to get back to her friends. Something had happened, something good, and she wanted to be in on it.

Chapter 44
Reunion

Echo was greeted at the door by Lucy, who immediately flung her arms around Echo. "Hi, Lucy. You look happy."

"I am." Lucy took Echo's hand and drew her into the common room where Dallas, Wilson, and the captain were sitting. Dallas stood up and gave Echo a hug, then Wilson followed suit. When they were done greeting her, the captain stood and placed her hands on Echo's shoulders.

"Welcome back, Echo," she said. And then the captain gently hugged her. "You look different," she said as she released Echo and looked into her eyes.

"I feel different," said Echo, but the captain didn't question her.

"I'm glad you've decided to stay with the Stewart crew," she said.

"Me too. But I'm going to take some classes in my spare time."

"Good idea." The captain turned to the others.

After an awkward silence, Wilson asked Echo if she would like something to drink.

"Just water."

"What? You've given up cola?" he teased.

Echo smiled. "Not completely. Water just sounds good right now."

Over dinner, Dallas told Echo about the house she had found. "There are two USSA guys living there, and they need two more people to share the rent. I thought you and I could move in."

"Well, I'd like to see the house and meet the guys, but it sounds promising."

Dallas clapped her hands together. "Great! We can go see it after dinner, if you have the time, that is," she said cautiously.

"Sure."

"Dana and Coop are getting married," Lucy blurted out.

"So I've heard," said Echo. She gave each of them a warm smile. "When's the wedding?"

"Soon," said Coop. "I have to find out when everyone is free. I wouldn't want any of mine or Dana's crew to miss out. We want Cheyenne to be able to come, and of course, your mother and Jeremy are welcome too."

"Thank you," said Echo. "So, I hear we'll be using Nellis as our base from now on," she said to no one in particular.

"That's right," said the captain. "I have requested four Mars trips a year. I hope no one minds. Of course, anyone on my team is free to join another team if they find an opening. I want to be home more." She winked at Lucy who grinned back at her.

To Echo, that was a relief. She didn't want to go on so many trips anyway. She could use the in between time to work at her mother's store and take classes. She still did eventually want to be a spaceplane pilot—when she was ready to leave the Stewart team.

"Dallas?"

"I'll stay with you," she said to the captain. "Four trips a year is okay with me. Between trips, I'll find some other type of work that is *not* loading nuclear waste into rockets."

"You could sub on other teams," Wilson offered.

Dallas raised her eyebrows. "That's an idea."

The rental house that Dallas had found was spacious with five bedrooms and three facilities. Two of the bedrooms were downstairs while three were upstairs. And the house had a basement as well. It was old and had some earthquake damage, but the guys who lived there were repairing the roof and installing seismic bracing. The house was government owned with an option to buy.

Dallas and Echo chose the downstairs bedrooms. The rent for each occupant was a hundred and fifty dollars a month, but if they got another roommate, the rent would go down slightly. And then there was the utility bill on top of that, but Echo figured she could afford it as long as she kept working at her mother's store between space trips. Overall, she was happy with the location of the house, which was about halfway between her mother's store and Captain Stewart's house. Plus, she had her vehicle. Most the electric highways had been restored, so she didn't have to rely on her car's battery as much.

The wedding was held outside on a hill with a view of the city. Almost everyone the couple had invited was able to attend. Echo's mother didn't come, nor did Cheyenne's father, but Cheyenne came. Echo hadn't seen her in over a year, and she seemed more grownup and less eccentric. Echo greeted her warmly with a hug. In fact, she couldn't remember when she had hugged so many people in one day. Sanders even made an appearance.

Captain Stewart wore a sky blue silk pants suit, and Wilson wore a traditional navy blue suit. She stood slightly taller than he, but he didn't appear bothered by that at all. The ceremony was short. No vows were spoken except they agreed to stay together as long as they both wanted to. To Echo, that made sense. A justice of the peace pronounced them husband and wife, then they kissed, keeping with tradition. The audience cheered.

The warm May afternoon went by quickly, as the guests and the newlyweds ate and drank and danced to a live band. As the sun lowered into the western sky, Echo was struck by the clarity of the air. She and Dallas moved to the edge of the cliff. Wilson and the captain joined them. Lucy ran up and inserted herself between the captain and Wilson, taking each of their hands. Then Echo felt Dallas gently brush her hand. Echo took it. Standing next to the captain, she also took her hand. The five of them stood at the edge of the cliff, in a kind of timeless moment, and watched the sun set behind a clear Los Angeles sky.

THE END